INDIANAPOLIS

First Uncle B. Publications printing, April 2025
        2   3   4   5   6   7   8   9   10

Previous publications of the stories contained within this volume appeared in *Sycamore Lane*, *Killer Tales*, *Pulp Modern*, and *The Magnolia Review*.

ISBN: 978-1-957034-24-9

BEAUTIFUL TERROR:

Science Fiction
and
Horror Stories

By
Stanley Rutgers

Beautiful Terror:

THE PITY MONSTER

Henry Mould and his daughter Betty pulled up around six, just in time for supper. Kate Mould ran out to greet them. As soon as her little girl stepped from the truck, she grabbed her and squeezed her.

"How's my baby!"

Betty pushed her mom away. "It's only been a semester."

Henry gathered his daughter's two suitcases and directed the family toward the house, suggesting she carry the smaller piece.

Betty looked around the farm and smiled. "It's so quaint."

Henry and Kate exchanged a confused glance. "What'you mean by that, pumpkin?" Henry asked.

"I'm meeting people from all over the world, Pa. They're telling me about cities where you don't see two patches of grass in the same square mile."

Henry watched his daughter's eyes picture a town bigger than Stockton. "You know them folks in the city is soulless, right?"

Betty hit her father on the chest. "Don't be so old fashioned!" She ran into the house, allowing her father to carry her luggage for her.

Henry turned to his wife. "I told you they'd puddin' up her mind at that university."

His wife took his arm into hers and rubbed his shoulders. "Relax, Papa Bear. Your daughter is the first Mould to go to college. Let's be happy."

Henry sighed. "Okie-dokie."

Henry, Kate, and Betty sat down and began eating home grown vegetables and a chicken slaughtered that very day. Betty watched her father dig in, disgust coloring her face.

"What's wrong, dear?" Kate asked.

"I don't eat meat anymore."

Between bites, Henry asked, "You lose all your teeth at school?"

Kate laughed.

"I'm a vegetarian."

"We got plenty of vegetables. Help yourself."

Betty pushed her plate away. "I can't consume animal flesh."

Henry stopped eating. "Young lady..."

The sound of Walter, the family's old bull, sticking it to an intruder and calling for help tore the calm air outside.

Henry stood. "Let me get my shotgun."

Kate put her hand over her mouth. The last time someone had trespassed on their farm Henry had almost put bullets into a hippy looking for psychedelic mushrooms. "Henry," she said as she chased after him.

"Great," Betty said. "I come home to an orgy of bloodshed."

With a lantern dangling from the end of the rifle, Henry approached the fenced in area Walter and three cows called home. He could make out the bull, trying to stomp on someone rolling around in the dirt. Two cows stood in the corner. Another lay on its side. Even in the dark, Henry could see a healthy chunk of flesh had been removed from the dead one.

"Whoever you are," he said, "I'ma make you pay, one way or another, for fellin' my livestock."

Kate and Betty approached him. They saw the carnage and slowed their approach.

Henry walked to the fence. "Walter! You get now. I'll take care of it."

Walter continued trampling on the intruder.

Henry took the lantern off the barrel of the gun, held it in a free hand and fired into the dirt. His wife and daughter jumped back. Walter charged over to the cows.

The stranger, whoever it was, lay still on the ground. Walter had done a number on him or her.

Henry crept up, shotgun ready, and held the light out over the fence. Staring back at him was a sickly gray creature the likes of an ugliness he had never seen. It was relatively small, though it had claws as sharp as razors and teeth the size of butcher knives. If you took the nastiest little fox, Henry thought, and skinned it, you still couldn't fashion a more unattractive beast. The thing grinned, revealing chunks of cow flesh and blood in its mouth. It tried moving, growling, but instead groaned in pain.

"You demonic summa'bitch." Henry raised the rifle to put one between its eyes.

"Pa…" Betty grabbed the barrel of the shotgun and turned it toward the ground.

Never taking his eyes off the creature, Henry forced himself to speak in a polite voice. "Pumpkin, would you please let your daddy take care of the farm?"

"You don't know what that is," Betty said, "you can't just kill it."

Henry aimed once more for the monster.

Betty jumped onto and over the fence and stood between the creature and her father.

"Get your hind out' the way!" said Henry.

"I won't let you kill it," said Betty.

Kate said, "Reckon Stockton police ain't big enough to handle this. That's a, I don't know what… Maybe some scientists from Lincoln might tell us."

"Kate," said Henry, "let me handle this."

Betty shook her head. "You call the scientists, the government, they'll cut this poor little thing up, study it like a frog."

"Maybe it needs to be studied," Kate said.

"They can study its corpse," said Henry. "Get out of the way!"

Betty knelt down in front of the creature, looked it over. "It—and I hope I don't offend it by calling it `it,'— but it needs to be nursed back to health."

"It," said Henry, "needs to die."

Betty crawled through the mud to the beast. The creature did not attack her. "See," she said, "this little, ah, whatever, wouldn't hurt a fly."

"That damned thing killed my livestock."

"You kill animals every day," said Betty. "How are you any less a monster?"

Kate took a napkin from her pocket and wiped her forehead. She rubbed her husband's shoulders. "We'll keep it in the old barn. Let Betty take care of it while she's here."

Henry shook his head. He looked at his daughter, who nodded in agreement with her mother's suggestion. "This is crazy. That thing's obviously a killer..."

"Gandhi," said Betty.

"What?"

"I've named it Gandhi, so we can stop calling it `it'."

Henry shrugged. "Guess I'm outnumbered."

"Thank you, Pa!"

Henry handed the shotgun to Kate. "Let me get some gloves," he said. "You keep the barrel on the little summa'bitch while I carry it to the barn."

"Pa!" Betty said. "You're gonna' offend it."

Walking away, Henry muttered, "Why am I paying thousands of dollars a semester to have her brain wiggled silly?"

Kate kept the shotgun high while Henry, doing his best to hold his nose, carried Gandhi into the old barn, just to the right of the newer, larger structure he built while his daughter was in high school. Betty followed them with the expression of a child who had just been given her first allowance.

"Should he get healthy before the end of winter break, I want to take him back to school with me," she said.

Henry grunted, dropped the creature onto the floor and started speaking when Kate interrupted:

"Let's just wait and see if the poor thing even makes it through the night."

Looking around, Henry spotted a dog chain he used for Polly, the family's German Shepherd that died just before Betty turned eighteen. He hammered a nail into a u-shape, securing the chain to the wall, and put the choker around Gandhi's neck.

"What are you doing that for?" said Betty.

"Now, now," said Kate. "Papa Bear's just protecting the livestock."

"That is so cruel!"

"This thing," Henry started—

"Gandhi," his daughter said.

"It is to be on this chain at all times." He looked his daughter in the eyes, let her know how serious he was. "The door to the barn is to be barred on the outside. If he gets out once—I mean once—I will put him down faster than a wild dog on a rabbit, you understand?"

Betty folded her arms, craned her head in effort to avoid her father's gaze.

"Young lady?"

"You're a fascist."

Henry grabbed her arm and pulled her in close. "You ain't too old to be bent over a knee."

"Oh my God!" said Betty.

Kate stepped in, pushed Henry away from their daughter. "This is no way to celebrate Christmas," she said. "Let's get back to dinner."

Betty rushed into the old barn early the next morning with a plate of carrots. The creature, stained with its own blood, woke up, felt its pain and winced while Betty shoved carrots at its face. It chomped a piece off of one and spit it back out.

"All right," she said. "I'll get you some meat."

After a debate with her father, who once again suggested killing the creature was the easiest solution, Betty convinced him to give her two steaks from the cooler in the basement. She ran back to the old barn and slid the beef under Gandhi's nose.

It sniffed at the meat and then ate both steaks in quick, nervous bites. The primitive display shocked Betty into scooting away.

"You don't seem to have good table manners," she said, "but I'm not gonna' judge you for that." She reached out to pet it. The beast snapped at her hand and growled. "Bad Gandhi!" she said. "If you want more food, just ask."

The creature panted like a dog, licked old and new chunks of meat from around its mouth.

"Ok." Betty went back to the house.

Once more, she fought with Henry to get Gandhi some food.

"It's a special life-form," she said. "We have to nurture it."

"It's a filthy monster," Henry said.

"Ma!"

"Henry," her mother said, "remember, it's only for the break.

Betty watched Gandhi gobble up two more steaks. Again, the creature growled at her.

"That's hardly a way to thank someone for being nice," she said, waving a finger at it. "Maybe you just don't know any other way to ask for what you want."

As she stepped out of the old barn, she saw her father shoveling away what few inches of snow had fallen on the half mile driveway leading to the farm. "Really?" she said. "He can't just let nature be nature." Then she realized her father was not guarding the beef. Running to the house, she ducked into the basement and took five slabs from the ice box.

Gandhi ate the first four with the same ferocity as the previous helpings. The fifth slowed it down. By the time it was finished, it rolled to its side and let out a sound Betty assumed was a burp.

She put her hand on its belly. The creature did not protest.

"There," she said, "I knew you were harmless. You just needed to be fed." She brushed away flakes of blood that had dried on its leathery skin. "I'll make you all better," she said, "and I'll see to it that Herr Pa' never points a gun at your little head again."

Gandhi groaned, licked its lips and stared at her. It made a small gesture towards her, sniffing, like, then laid back and closed its eyes.

Betty ran her fingers over the chains holding it hostage. "Pa's such a monster," she scowled. Looking over her shoulder, she moved towards the link holding the shackles to the wall. Her father had staked it good. She couldn't pull it out with her bare hands. "Don't you worry," she said.

"You got a phone call," Kate said to her daughter as she entered the kitchen for lunch. "A fellow referring to himself as," she winced as she said the name, "Dragon."

Betty grabbed the phone off the wall and dialed.

Kate watched her while she stirred a bowl of black beans and rice.

"Dragon?" Betty's voice carried an electric excitement. "Dude, I thought I was gonna' die here in the 1800s house."

Kate shook her head and began setting the table.

"Nine? Sure, I'll see you then."

As she put plates on the table, Kate asked, "That your boyfriend?"

"One of them," Betty said. Noting her mother's worried look, she laughed. "I'm not settling down, Ma, I'm not making the same mistake you made."

Kate stood back, studied her daughter for signs of sarcasm. No joke, she realized, and fired back—"Exactly what mistake did I make?"

Betty rolled her eyes. "Gimme' a break. You're Pa's slave."

Leaning forward, shaking a fist in her daughter's face, Kate whispered, "Your Pa's not the only one'll hand you a spell."

Betty said "What'd you wanna be when you were a little girl, Ma?"

"I'm doing exactly what I always wanted to do." She walked away, calling for her husband.

Henry and Kate Mould sat in their living room reading magazines. He looked over a Time while his wife finished off the latest Reader's Digest. Both jumped when a loud knock fell on the front door.

"Oh yeah," Kate said. "Betty's got a date."

Henry raised a brow. "The Polk boy, the one she was seeing last year? Summa'bitch tore a hamstring. `Don't think he'll ever play pro."

Shaking her head, Kate said, "I don't think so."

The stairs rocked as Betty bounced down them and snapped the door open.

"Betty?" Henry was up and approaching the door.

Betty peeked back in, "What?"

Henry opened the door and took a good look at the boy on the other side.

Seth "Dragon" Harland, lanky, dressed in a torn T-shirt, jeans, boots and no jacket, stared back at Henry. A cigarette dangled from his mouth. He smiled and offered his hand.

Henry took Dragon's hand and shook it until the boy realized he could not match the old man's grip. "Why you got cartoons on your arm, son?"

Betty sounded as though she were a tire relieved of its air. "Really? Those are tattoos, Pa."

Henry smiled at Seth. "Betty's curfew is midnight."

"Pa!" She stomped her foot on the ground, then pushed past Dragon. "Come on," she said.

Dragon remained on the porch, unsure whom he should appease.

"Midnight, son, otherwise I'll erase them cartoons with a blow torch and straight-razor." Henry shut the door on the boy's face.

Setting their alarm clock for seven in the morning, the Moulds covered up to sleep. Henry kissed his wife, then rolled to his side and shut his eyes.

A shriek kept them from sleeping. A piercing sound, suggesting someone scraping his teeth down the side of a fence post and screaming at the same time.

Sitting up, Henry looked at the clock. "Don't tell me the girl forgot to feed that…thing."

Kate rubbed her eyes and yawned. "She's a young woman, Henry, can't keep calling her a girl."

"What does that have to do with anything?"

"Just feed it."

"I got a better idea."

Kate threw her covers off. "I'll do it then, shoot." She pushed her feet into her slippers and pulled her nightgown in closer.

Henry stood up. ""I don't want you getting tore up by that thing."

Both dressed for the cold air outside and headed to the cellar.

11

As they approached the old barn, Gandhi's cries forced them to cover their ears. Henry carried two slabs of beef and a mouth turned in disgust after having witnessed how much food the beast had already eaten.

"This thing doesn't die soon we're gonna' be out of fixins' before the New Year."

"You can take down the other cows if you have to." Kate lifted the latch on the barn and opened the door. She raised the only lantern they brought to make light for Henry as he stepped through.

He started unwrapping the meat, then looked at the floor of the barn. From his count, Betty had already given up ten cuts. "Darn it, Kate, you see what she's doing?"

The creature cried again. Kate covered her ears, sending the light to the ceiling.

"Sweetheart," Henry said, "last thing I need is that summa'bitch tearing my hand off." He threw the first slab to Gandhi.

They watched it eat in its nervous manner.

"It looks like something out of that old Jason and the Argonauts movie." Henry tossed the other piece of beef and turned to leave.

Kate followed. Before they were through the door, however, Gandhi shrieked once more.

Henry turned around. "How about I yank that tongue out of your mouth?"

Kate put herself between her husband and Gandhi. "Go get some more meat."

Henry moved his head left to right.

Kate raised her eyebrows. "Would you like to try sleeping while this, this whatever, cries all night?"

Looking towards the sky, as though God might drop down and give him a hand in the matter, Henry turned and headed back for the house. "Just holler if he gets out of hand."

12

THE PITY MONSTER

Kate ignored her husband and knelt down close to the creature. She tried petting it, but it snapped at her. Raising the lantern to get a look at its eyes, she saw that it was shaking. Tears streamed down the sides of its face. "You poor little thing," she said. "Papa Bear's gonna' take care of you, don't you worry."

Gandhi growled and chomped at her again.

Jumping back, Kate scolded the beast. "That's not friendly at all."

Henry returned. "Here you go." He threw two more chunks of beef at the monster. He held his wife while they watched it eat.

After the final piece, Gandhi rolled to its side. Kate knelt down next to it and patted its belly.

"Kathryn Lucinda Mould, what in creation are you doing?"

Shushing her husband, Kate eased into a gentle caress of the beast's rough hide.

Gandhi did not protest. The creature looked at her and licked its lips.

"I think it likes me."

"How you can even put your hand on that nasty summa'bitch is well beyond me." Henry prayed to God he wasn't about to get cursed with two bleeding hearts under his roof.

"Is Lincoln in a different time zone?" Henry didn't even touch his breakfast before laying into his daughter.

Betty stopped, fork in mid-air. "What are you talking about?"

"I heard you come in at one."

"Henry…" Kate nodded towards the food on his plate.

"I am a woman, I can do what I want." Betty shoved a pile of eggs in her mouth before she said anymore.

"While you live in my house," Henry pointed his fork at her, "you obey my rules."

Kate sighed. She looked out the kitchen window, hoping something magnificent would happen and divert her family's attention.

"You have always been a tyrant, Pa." Betty took a sip of orange juice, continued—"you insisted I learn how to hunt when I was twelve, even though I told you I didn't like guns, let alone shooting 'em. You made me go to Lincoln with you to watch the Huskers even though I hate football. Can I please have my own life now?"

"When you pay your own bills or get smart enough to marry a fellow, a nice fellow, that is, who'll support you..."

"Marriage is slavery."

"Watch your tongue, girl."

Clearing her throat, Kate lifted a plate with bacon on it and offered it to her husband.

"Anyway, Dragon's taking me out again tonight and I don't want to hear about any goddamn curfew."

Henry's fist landed on the table, sending every plate a half inch into the air. "Young lady, you ain't too old to have a bar of soap run through your mouth. Besides, I don't understand what a big time city rat like, ah, Gorgon, or whatever you call him, I don't get why a boy's willing to drive sixty miles two nights in a row when," he stopped himself, looked at his daughter.

Betty glared back.

"Sweetheart," Kate said to her daughter, "could you make sure you feed that thing in the barn before you go out? Your father and I had to pick up the slack last night. You can guess how happy that made Papa Bear."

"I fed Gandhi."

"Well," Kate said, "he was sure hungry again."

"Then I guess he eats four meals."

Henry sat back, rubbed the bridge of his nose. "If the monster needs to eat twice at night, you can't go out."

Now Betty's fist landed on the table, sending the dishes almost as high.

"Henry, Henry," said Kate, "it's ok, really. If the, Gandhi, or whatever, needs to be fed again I'll take care of it."

"I don't want you going near that rodent by yourself."

Betty spoke through a mouthful of pancakes—"Could you stop treating the women in this family like children?"

Henry leaned towards his daughter. "Before I shuffle off this here mortal coil," he said, "I hope you can find it in your heart to someday forgive me for turning you into such a brat."

Kate clicked her tongue. "Henry..."

Gandhi screamed for food around one in the afternoon. Without asking her father's permission, Betty took five slabs of meat out to the old barn. The creature's wounds had healed and, like a cat, it had licked itself clean.

"You're all better," she said, kneeling down to pet it.

Gandhi snapped at her, then sniffed like a dog for food.

"Here you go." Betty threw the meat all at once onto the floor.

The beast gobbled it up and then rolled over on its side. Once more, Betty knelt down to caress it. Gandhi breathed deep, satisfied breaths. It craned its head around, sniffed at Betty's hand and licked her fingers.

"That's a good Gandhi," she said, trying not to giggle from the tickling the creature's tongue provided. She stroked its belly and said, "You're harmless." Looking at the chain in the wall, she decided she would liberate the animal and then choose an outfit for her date.

"That is one sweet-looking moon," Dragon stared towards the sky as he drove.

"Keep your eyes on the road," Betty said.

Dragon looked at her, from her smooth legs straight up to beautiful face. She was in a black mini-skirt she wore

15

at school whenever she needed to convince a professor to excuse her from a test. How she got out of her house with it on was a mystery he would save for another night. "Is there a clearing around here, somewhere we can park?"

Betty sighed, glanced out the window at the distant lights of downtown Stockton. "We're not far away enough from hell. Just drive."

"I have something I want to tell you." Dragon pulled the car over and turned the engine off. "Betty," he leaned in close, "I've been doing a lot of thinking."

"I doubt you even know the meaning of the word."

"I'm being serious." He took a deep breath. "I love you. I love you and I wanna' marry you."

Silence filled the car. He turned the radio on. Through the static, a Lincoln rock station played a Fleetwood Mac song.

"Is this a joke?" Betty curled her hands into fists.

"Come on, baby..."

"Turn the damn car around and take me home."

"Betty, don't be like this."

"I swear, I'll scream!"

Dragon sat back, cranked the engine and peeled out.

As Henry and Kate prepared for bed, Gandhi cried to the night once more. Kate put her shoes on and headed for the door.

"I'll come with you, hold on." Henry rolled his socks back over his ankles.

"It's really not necessary."

"I don't want you going around that thing all by your lonesome."

Kate laughed. "Henry Mould, was this world safe before you came along?"

Throwing his arms up, Henry relented.

As Kate rummaged through the cooler for meat, she noticed Henry's hammer and crowbar lying on the ground. "That's not like you, Papa Bear," she said as she hung the tools back up. Clutching four slabs of meat, she headed for the old barn.

"Baby..." Dragon continued the effort to break through the wall of ice Betty had built around her.

"What did I tell you?" Betty said. "When we met at Kohli's party, remember?"

"Of course I remember. That was the most special night of my life."

"You idiot. It was just sex. It's just sex, what we do, it means nothing, don't you get it?" Her eyes narrowed. "Are you really this uncool? Really?"

Gandhi's cries were louder than usual. Kate hurried, afraid Henry might come down and kick the beast one time to shut it up. She nudged the door to the barn open and slid inside. The weight of the meat became too much. She dropped the packages.

"Fudge," she said, then groped for a dangling light bulb she wasn't even sure worked. When she found it, she felt something pass between her legs. "Just relax," she said. She flipped the switch and the barn lit up just enough for Kate to see the empty choker that had once contained Gandhi.

Kate Mould's scream drowned the shrieks of the beast. She called for her husband and then God as the creature sprang onto her throat and dug its teeth into her flesh.

Henry was outside before he could even think to put on his shoes.

Ripping open the door to the old barn, he saw Gandhi, covered in his wife's blood, sitting on her chest and chewing at a wound cut into her neck. "Son of a bitch!" He leapt and rolled with the beast off of Kate's dying body.

Using all his strength, he held the monster's jaws away from his face. "Dear Lord," he said, "answer this one prayer."

"Pa?"

Henry whipped his head from side to side, insuring his daughter was not a near-death hallucination. When he opened his eyes again, he saw her standing in the doorway, moonlight illuminating her from behind. For the first time since she had been a little girl, she looked just like an angel.

"Go get daddy's shotgun from the coat closet, hurry!"

Betty surmised the situation, hesitated, then ran back to the house.

"Please Lord…" Henry continued struggling to keep the beast from tearing his throat out.

Betty returned with the rifle. Remembering what her Pa had taught her when she was twelve, she checked it for shells, wracked it and aimed. She squinted and then pulled the trigger.

Her young eyes delivered a shot straight to her father's brain.

(2004)

PHOBIAPHOBIA

Stan Belly was minding his own business, seated on the toilet, reading the *Wall Street Journal*. His mind was entrenched in figuring out whether to panic over his sole stock investment dipping three percent from the previous day's report.

A mouse jumped out from behind the toilet, scurried to the wall and then underneath the door and into the hallway. Stan's mind hadn't processed the rodent's presence until just before it flattened itself and squeezed under the door. It took another fraction of second before Stan jumped up and shouted, "Dammit!"

He rolled up his newspaper and threw it at the door.

What followed was his usual embarrassment at having been scared by something so tiny and insignificant. He finished his job on the toilet with his feet raised above the ground, should another mouse show up. Then he stormed into his boss's office.

"We got mice again."

Andrew Miller sighed, laid the report he was pretending to read on his desk. "Stan," he said, "you're a grown man. Can't you live with the occasional mouse running around?"

"It's unsanitary."

"It's unavoidable. This building is located between a construction site and a strip mall filled with food joints that dump their scraps in the alley. We're lucky it's just mice."

The thought of the mouse's evil cousins, rats, invading the building sent a chill down Stan's spine that made his entire body quake. "I see a rat," he announced, "I'm quitting."

Andrew stood and paced. "Stan, you can't quit your job over some rodents. That doesn't make any sense."

"I'm not the only one who doesn't like mice."

"I know. At least three of the twelve women employed here scream when they see one."

"What are you saying?"

"Stan, you're afraid of everything. You take the stairs because you're claustrophobic. You're the most ridiculous germ-a-phobe I've ever seen."

"Excuse me?"

"You carry your own roll of paper towels to the bathroom and kitchen. You disinfect your computer keyboard every morning, despite the fact that we have an excellent clean up crew that does that at night."

"Who knows what happens between the time they clean and the time I get in here in the morning?"

"But you spray the keyboard even if you've been away from your desk for two minutes."

"Germs are..." He sank his head. His boss was right. Everyone was right. His parents, his ex-wife, his children.

Andrew sat back down at his desk and pulled a black, leather notebook out of one of the drawers. He flipped through it until he found what he was looking for. He picked up his phone and dialed, waited. "Yes, hello," he spoke into the receiver. "I'd like to make an appointment for today, if possible. Three? Sounds great. My name is Stan Belly. That's right, Belly, like stomach, Belly." He hung up.

"What's going on, Andrew?"

Stan wrote an address on a blank note card. "You're going to see a hypnotherapist. Have her hypnotize you into being a man." He handed him the card.

"I take offense..."

"Get your brain fixed, Stan, or find somewhere else to work."

Stan stood still.

"What are you waiting for?" Andrew motioned for him to leave.

"What if I prove..." He thought about it, then snapped his fingers. "I'll ride the elevator."

Andrew shook his head. "That's not going to do the trick. I need you to work and not worry about stuff nobody else worries about." He pointed once more to the door. "I got things to do, Stan."

* * *

Stan stared at the elevator doors for a long, long time. His coworkers got in and out of the deadly contraption without thinking about it. Stan pitied them in the beginning. Then he tried to step in it. As soon as the doors started to close, he hit the 'Open Door' button and jumped out.

Before long, Stan's pity turned into respect. Everyone had been right. He was weak. He gave up on the elevator and took the stairs to the ground level. After spraying disinfectant over the door handle on his car, he opened it, got in and drove to the address his boss had provided.

Dr. Karen Glass's office looked exactly like the one Stan visited weekly as a child. In those days, however, the treatment was good old fashioned psychotherapy. Dr. Glass was an attractive woman, long dark hair, sharp, curious eyes lurking over the rims of "smart-and-sexy-girl" glasses. She sat at her desk with her chin rested over the tops of her hands.

"Do you think I'm right, and everyone else is wrong?" Stan tried a final time to convince at least one other person that there was nothing odd about his behavior.

"You tell me." Dr. Glass smiled politely.

Stan shrugged.

"Mr. Belly, you disinfected that chair before you sat down in it."

"I don't know who's been sitting here."

"And you feel you might be normal, and the rest of us have simply failed to catch on?"

Stan bowed his head. "I'm crazy."

Dr. Glass stood and walked around her desk. She put her hand on Stan's shoulder. "We don't use that word here, Mr. Belly. You have panophobia."

He looked up, confused.

"You're afraid of everything."

She was right. Stan knew it. For the first time someone had summed up his neurosis in four tidy words. He nodded.

Dr. Glass smiled. "The good news is, I can cure you right here and now." She proceeded to hypnotize Stan Belly.

"From now on," she said, while Stan was under her influence, "anything that made you afraid in the past will now make you laugh. You'll find endless joy in anything you once felt frightening."

She snapped her fingers and Stan Belly's mind climbed out of its subconscious cellar.

"Shall we test the treatment?"

"I guess." Stan was unaware any treatment had taken place.

Dr. Glass walked into a room located to the side of her office. She came back with a small metal cage. Inside was a rat the size of a rabbit.

Stan's initial thought was to stand and run like hell. It was quickly quelled by something he didn't quite recognize. "Wh, what are you doing?"

Dr. Glass opened the cage, pulled the rat out and tossed it to Stan.

Instead of putting his hands up to bat the creature down, Stan opened them and caught the animal. Every fiber in his body wanted to scream. He opened his mouth and out came...

Laughter.

Stan laughed like no human being had ever laughed before. It was loud, liberating. The sound came from the bottom of his stomach and bounced off the wooden floor and walls of the office. The rat became anxious and bit Stan's finger.

"Oh," Dr. Glass took the beast away and put it back in its cage. "I'm so sorry," she said, looking around for something to bandage the wound. "I swear, he doesn't have rabies."

Stan waved off her concern. He stood up. "Don't worry about it," he said. "I'll have my regular doctor look at it next time I go in for a check up. Speaking of checks, whom do I pay?"

"Your boss is footing the bill."

"That's great." Stan patted the doctor on her back. "I'll show myself out." He felt like he might choke on his own confidence.

As Stan walked to his car in the parking lot, a young man dressed in a jeans jacket, jeans, and baseball cap, strolled up behind him. He wore a blue scarf over the bottom of his face, much the way bandits in old cowboy movies did.

"Pop that wallet," said the young man.

Stan chuckled. "I'm afraid I'm not familiar with your slang."

"Give me your goddamned wallet," the stranger said. He pulled out a .9mm and pointed it at Stan's side.

Seeing the gun caused a tidal wave of laughter from Stan.

"What the hell's so goddamn funny?"

"I'm not," Stan tried to catch his breath between laughs, "I'm not going to give you my wallet."

"What?" The thuglet rammed the barrel of the gun into Stan's stomach.

"It doesn't belong to you." He was almost crying from the hilarity of the situation.

"Give me your goddamn wallet or I'll drop you right here."

This was too much. Stan fell to his knees. The humor was unbearable.

The little criminal lost his patience. He shot Stan in the back of the head, rummaged though his pockets for his wallet and anything else that might be valuable. Then he left him there to bleed and laugh himself to death.

(2005)

THE PROBLEM REMOVER

Are you dissatisfied with your life? Family weighing you down? Financial woes giving you nightmares? At Problem Removal, Inc., we make it possible for you to erase every glitch life has thrown your way. You'll be a brand new person before you know it!

I've found the key to success is routine. Some might call it habit. Those destined for crime or insanity would no doubt refer to my prescription as boring. That's fine. I live in a three story house by the ocean. They live in a corporate jail or commercial mental facility. Of course, they've been convinced that life is perfect when someone else takes care of you. I know better. I'm one of the clever souls who make it possible for the War on Freedom to work.

Let's face it, life in the 21st Century, life in the American Union, is not really a life for anyone who can't afford to make money off of other people's misery. Only the most clever enjoy an existence that, at the very least, provides the illusion of freedom.

My alarm clock rings, even though it's not necessary, precisely at five o'clock in the morning every single day. I get up, dress in my gym clothes and work out for exactly one hour and a half. After a shower and shave, I prepare breakfast: A protein shake and two raw eggs.

My wife Barbara wakes up right around the time I leave for work. Her job is to shop. Occasionally I need her for social gatherings. She knows how to make herself prettier than any other woman in the room. This makes me look wealthier, which is vital. You cynics might refer to her as "arm candy."

I leave for the office at seven-thirty. Monday through Friday. On Saturdays I take my wife to the Santa Monica Consumer Hall and spend massive amounts of money on things we never use or need. On Sundays we go to church for salvation and entertainment. My name is Greg Geist. I am a

Problem Remover. Before the time of the Union, I might have been called doctor, or preacher.

Nine out of ten Problem Removers recommend Schizodein for your multiple-personality needs. Beneficial side effects include hallucinations, conversations with people who don't exist, and a guarantee that you will be spending the rest of your life in a luxurious corporate mental facility. Schizodein, a product of Shamgen Chemicals.

On Monday my first client was a young woman named Helen. She believed that her husband was cheating on her. They had produced two children, despite the fact that their credit rating was not above 900.

"That was your first mistake," I said to her.

"I know, I know."

"Poor people should not reproduce."

"I know."

She looked like she felt a sufficient amount of guilt. She told me she didn't want to face her husband or have the children exposed to such a messy circumstance. Better to just disappear in a corporate-sponsored institution.

Criminality was not appropriate in her case. I suggested a nervous breakdown. Two companies manufactured excellent drugs for just such a treatment.

"My sister went that route," she said, "I'd like to do something no one in my family has done yet."

"Have you considered depression?"

Helen smiled. "Depression sounds interesting."

"Very good," I said, writing a prescription for pills that would eliminate her brain's ability to produce endorphins. "Take these until you feel completely miserable, then check yourself into a mental facility. I recommend the Permanent Vacation Spa in Anaheim."

"Thank you." She shook my hand and left.

THE PROBLEM REMOVER

On Tuesday it was an AU Citizen of African Descent. He was worried because he enjoyed both classical music and old novels by Louise L'amour. This was an obvious violation of the culture quota, which stated one could only prefer a single element of a community other than his own.

"Because your ancestors came from Africa," I explained, "it's difficult to get you into a mental facility. Are you prepared for prison?"

"They feed you, right?"

"Of course."

"Every day?"

I nodded.

"What's the difference between prison and a mental facility?"

"An asylum provides the illusion of freedom. Prison is more honest."

Howard, that was the gentlemen's name, sighed. "I'm an honest guy," he said.

"No problem, Howard." I prescribed a car-jacking. All crimes now carried the same penalty. One arrest would earn you a life sentence. There would be a trial, but that was only so judges and lawyers could continue to get paid. Defendants were always found guilty in the American Union.

Howard assured me he would purchase a gun (I recommended an excellent shop where he could buy an unregistered firearm under the table) and rob a rich person within the next twenty-four hours.

My brother Phil was a lawyer. I gave Howard his business card and promised him Phil would provide a wonderfully incompetent defense that would get him thrown in jail without the hassle of an appeal.

Wednesday brought a young man, about twenty-three, to my office. Interesting case. He was still very much enthusiastic about recreational sex. This was a nasty violation of the Union's law against carnal pleasure. Procreation was, of course, accomplished through science. Test tubes and sterile rooms where men did their business and that business was passed on to women in other rooms. Very clean. Very pure.

"Intercourse is a most heinous crime," I said, shaking my head the way a father scolding a child might do, "it's how the Union almost failed, before it became the Union."

"Yeah, yeah," the boy said. His name was Chris. He told me he loved brunettes. "Dark haired women," he clarified, "I like their curves." Demonstrating what he meant, he made an imaginary hour-glass figure with his hands in the air. A smile that clearly begged for an insane solution unfolded across his face.

"This is a no-brainer," I concluded. "I suggest severe oedipal psychosis. You'll need to become a brutal serial killer and locked up in a high-security mental ward at a fine corporate prison."

The boy hid his enthusiasm with a look of fear. "I don't want to kill people. I just want to make love to women."

I pressed the panic button underneath my desk. Two guards entered and took Chris to the emergency room where he could be properly injected with a powerful mix of psychedelic drugs that would make him therapeutically psychotic.

Thursday's child was an AU Citizen of Asian Descent. Susan Choi. Her great-great grandparents had come to the Union from Korea. Susan was a friendly woman. Too much so. She had exceeded almost every social quota.

"I have three black friends, three white friends, and four Latino friends."

I cleared my throat and spoke. Susan was obviously not interested in Union Correctspeak. "You mean AU Citizens of African, European, and South American Descent, right?"

Susan refused to answer. She had been sent to the organization by her mother. 'Rebellious' was the word she used to describe her daughter. The very idea made me sick to my stomach.

"You realize your disregard for social quotas..."

"I don't want the government to tell me who I can and can't be friends with." She folded her arms, draped one leg over the other and kicked her free foot up and down impatiently.

"There is no more government, Susan."

"Corporation, government, what's the difference?"

Prison was too good for her. I called on the guards to take her in for a laser lobotomy. A simple process. A light with the force of a battering ram shot right through the center of her brain. She would spend the remainder of her mortal life as a vegetable at a third rate mental facility somewhere in the ruins of South Los Angeles.

The only remorse I felt was for her mother. Then I remembered I could just prescribe her a nice nervous breakdown and send her to a luxurious asylum in Malibu.

By the end of the week I had earned commissions from twelve corporate prisons and twenty-one mental facilities. A bit slow for me, but a positive step towards purging the Union of independent thinkers.

Does your teenager mope around the house? Seem like he or she has no direction in life? Do you frequently catch your teenager engaging in sexual acts by him or herself or, Law forbid, another person? Does your teenager talk back? Use abusive language? Listen to rhythmic, repetitive music that contains suggestive lyrics? Does your teenager use drugs for reasons other than their official purpose? Sounds like you have a troublemaker. We can fix your child with a steady diet of psychotropic drugs and psychological scare tactics. Call the Same Center for an estimate and get your house in the order you know it's required to be in. After all, no one wants to be different.

On Saturday I took Barbara shopping. It was our patriotic duty. The Santa Monica Consumer Hall had a sale, as they did every weekend, on square plastic containers that served no purpose but looked very nice on kitchen counters and other useless surfaces the rich had about their houses.

We purchased three the previous week, but Barbara insisted we buy more. I protested, forgetting that spending, not saving, was the order of the day.

"We can stack the boxes we buy this week on top of the ones we bought last week."

"What purpose would that serve?"

"It would make my friends jealous."

"Aren't these the same color as the ones we bought last week?"

"Yes. That's what makes it perfect. They are exactly like the ones we already have."

I sighed. I fought some more to protect the money in my wallet. Then she pulled out the death card:

"You're not hiding money from the Union, are you?"

Of course not. It was my job to earn it, hers to spend it. I handed over my credit chip and let her buy everything she wanted.

To maintain order within my own mind, I remembered that people who did not have a perfect credit score, as I did, were unable to enjoy AU culture at its finest:

Shopping.

Second only to church.

That night we went to a party at my boss's house. The finest Problem Removers in the Los Angeles area were present. The men discussed work.

"Any perverts this week?"

"Why would this week be any different?"

A round of laughter. Some of it forced, but nobody dared to call anyone else out for being combative. Problem

THE PROBLEM REMOVER

Removal was a brotherhood of sorts. We would never send up one of our own.

The women discussed the plastic boxes they had purchased earlier in the day.

"We now have four rows on the dining room table."

"Oh Janice, stop being such a show off!"

A round of tee-hee-hee's, all fake. Our wives hated us and we knew it. They wouldn't dare rebel, however, knowing how difficult it would be to find a new husband with a perfect credit rating.

This is Charlie. Charlie is an atheist. He doesn't believe in consequence. He's going to hell, he knows it, and he doesn't care. How close is Charlie to becoming a terrorist? Do you want to be the one who finds out when it's too late? Report all atheists or anyone you suspect of being an atheist to the nearest Problem Removal organization. This has been a public service announcement of the American Union. God bless you on your journey to the shopping mall.

Sunday was church day. I wore my nicest suit. Barbara covered herself from head to toe in a fine satin dress that drooped just enough to hide the fact that she still had fabulous curves. Curves I was not allowed to enjoy according to the law. Whenever we visited the Consumer Creation Center, I thought about actually touching her, feeling her warm skin, running my fingers through her dark hair. It generally took all of ten seconds to make my contribution to the official procreation process.

Church was downtown, the old football stadium. A brief sermon was followed by an entertaining game of Poor People Slaughter. We cheered on wealthy young gladiators as they chased mental patients around the old grid iron with weapons of their choice. No matter how fast or crafty the insane thought they were, the rich warriors eventually caught them and slaughtered them.

Service lasted for an hour. As we filed out, I stared at the blood-splattered ground and remembered to thank God I had a perfect credit rating.

The next week began as all others did. Thank God. On Monday I dealt with a woman who had grown tired of her husband. This selfish creature actually suggested getting a divorce. Rick, her husband, had the good sense to bring her to the organization.

She was obviously hysterical. I spoke to her in a quiet, rational voice. "Lisa, what seems to be the problem?"

"My life is boring." She was doing her best to hold back tears.

"Does Rick work and provide a house for you to live in?" She nodded.

"Does he take you shopping every weekend?"

"Yes." The sniffles were threatening to break out into a full display of outlawed emotion.

I smiled my finest condescending grin. "What could you possibly have to complain about?"

"I," she hesitated, looked at Rick, who stared right back like a father shaming his daughter at an abortion clinic, "I want a job."

Rick and I let out a simultaneous gasp. This was simply too much. The Union had made it clear that work was for men and shopping was for women. I had dealt with stubborn wives like Lisa before, however, and knew exactly how to diagnose and treat her.

"You suffer from phallic delusions."

"Excuse me?" This seemed to make the tears dry right back up.

"You were born a woman, but you wish you were born a man."

She shook her head. "That's not true."

Rick put his hand up to keep her quiet. "Honey, let the professional handle this." He nodded to me to continue.

THE PROBLEM REMOVER

"I'm going to prescribe an estrogen-depleting drug that will kick start menopause. In addition, I'd like you to begin using an amphetamine. A powerful one. I'll write a prescription for a few and you decide which one works best. You will have magnificent anxiety attacks for which there is no known cure. Your husband can then have you committed." I turned to Rick and said, "Might I recommend the old California Women's Rehabilitation Center in San Marin? It was recently bought by Shamgen Chemical. They have a work program there that will satisfy your wife's irrational desire to have a job."

Lisa did not look happy about all the effort her husband and I were prepared to make to save her. "I don't want to kick start..."

Rick put his hand over his wife's mouth. "Don't worry, Mr. Geist, I'll have her locked up in no time."

I smiled. "Have a nice day."

Tuesday was interesting. A mother brought her son, Clark, into my office. They were joined, for reinforcement, by Clark's first grade teacher. The feisty little seven-year-old, it appeared, could not sit still in class.

"He always wants to play," his mother complained.

"Fifteen minutes into our daily memorization exercises involving multiplication tables," said the teacher, Ms. Newkirk, "Clark begins looking around the classroom. I just know he's going to do something crazy if he doesn't get help."

Even in my office, Clark couldn't stop kicking his little legs up and down in the giant seat he occupied. He had a mischievous look in his eye, like he was the kind of child who might derive unethical pleasure chasing a squirrel around a park. Very, very aggressive.

"I'm familiar with boys like Clark, here," I said, "and I know just how to prevent them from unleashing their anger and aggression on the innocent world." I opened my desk drawer and brought out a sample of Rittleshitoxin, a complex

37

amphetamine that caused the heart to beat faster and, in effect, force a child to slow down in order to avoid myocardial infarction. Clever drug. I handed the sample to his mother. "Get him started on these right away."

The teacher cleared her throat. "How will that help me control my classroom?"

"The child's aggressive nature will eventually force its way to the surface. You will then be within your legal rights to have him off-tracked to a school for children with concentration problems." I smiled at Clark's mother, "Both of you will soon be free from this monster."

The women were relieved. Clark shot me a glare that made me thank God he would be locked up for the rest of his life.

Variety reared its ugly face on Wednesday. I got a call at the office just after lunch. My wife, it appeared, had been ritualistically murdered by a serial killer. A new guy. I was asked to come down to the Corporate Police station, downtown Los Angeles, and determine whether or not I was familiar in any way with the suspect.

Now, you cynics and pessimists who used to take up classroom space in universities and ink and paper in radical, left-wing newspapers like the *New York Times* and *Washington Post*, you might have yourself a good laugh. No doubt you will rub your chins in a pseudo-intellectual manner to demonstrate how fascinating you find the irony in the situation.

The man who killed my wife was none other than Chris, the kid I had treated for having an unhealthy sex drive the week before. Barbara was his third victim. The drugs had acted quickly. He saw her in the parking lot of the Santa Monica Consumer Hall, kidnapped her right in front of all the security cameras, raped and then stabbed her, repeatedly, with the very same syringe he had used to inject his daily dose of psychosis-inducing pharmaceuticals.

THE PROBLEM REMOVER

Yes, you may call it irony. But I'm an optimist. I saw opportunity where a criminal or lunatic would have seen tragedy. I'm a successful man and I have no need for sorrow.

By Friday, I had purchased a new wife. Her name was Betty. She was a lot like Barbara, though she preferred blue plastic boxes to the red ones Barbara had been partial to.

(2005)

ODE TO JOY

"You game?"

Influence. The man with the cigar projected it. Why? thought Hauser Pratt, professional Time Shadow. No sooner had the question appeared in his mind, his blue chip flashed and an electrical current shorted out his immediate memory. "What were we talking about?"

"Retrieval, in the red district. Don't think." The fat man across the desk spit out pieces of tobacco from his cigar.

Have I got a choice? *Zap!* "Let me discuss it with the wife."

Frank Boorhead chuckled. "The wife happy living in the Blue district?"

"Of course not." Hauser sat back. "I'll probably take it."

His boss shoved an envelope across the desk. "Contracts. Bring them to me tomorrow."

Lucy Pratt wore her blue skirt. She brought her legs up on the sofa, displaying her thighs in a manner similar to the actresses of old-world television. A documentary about the United Corporations of America before the revolution demonstrated how wives used to influence unscheduled conjugal appointments with their husbands. She enjoyed the nostalgia conjured by such a performance, though she could never let it produce the calculated effect it did a few years previous. Lucy and her husband did not have permission to schedule a conjugal appointment for another month. The blue chip in her wrist flashed and her mind temporarily shorted out.

Hauser entered the apartment, saw his wife, stared at her legs, and moved on to the kitchen. "Dinner?" he asked.

"Work?" Lucy pointed at the envelope underneath Hauser's arm.

He nodded. "Retrieval. Red district."

"That's dangerous," his wife said. "What's the reward?"

"Handsome," he said. "A couple more jobs like it and we might be able to move to the White district."

"Why'd you bring it home?" She sat up.

"I thought I should talk it over with you."

"Why?" She smiled, hoping that would ease a coherent and honest answer from her husband.

"Like you said, it's dangerous. I might get killed."

Lucy shrugged. "Moving into a higher credit level is worth the risk, don't you think?"

Before Hauser could answer, the blue chip in his wrist flashed.

"Whoops," Lucy giggled. She picked up the remote control for the entertainment unit and turned on the television. A cheerful woman dressed in blue delivered the bulletin of the day:

"Police raided the Red district in the latest skirmish in the War on Poverty. Two officers were injured. Officials refused to comment on the number of Red casualties."

Pictures of police beating Red district citizens filled the screen. Lucy shuddered. "They're so disgusting," she said. "Why don't they just accept their fate?"

Hauser sat down next to his wife, took the remote control and turned the news machine off. "How about dinner?"

Lucy sighed. The blue identity chip in her wrist blinked.

The scent of a naked woman had always surprised him. The flowers of society, as his father had raised him to regard them, smelled remarkably human once stripped of their fancy dresses, once sweat from passion washed off the artificial odors they splashed on their bodies. Chemicals in his mind prevented him from worrying about anything but getting as close to her as possible. He ran his hands over her skin, each second causing his blood to pump through his body faster and faster.

"God..." she said as his hands traced inside her thighs. She returned the gesture and they wrapped their legs around each other.

"I'm so in love with you," he whispered.

She urged him on top of her. Once he slipped inside, both moaned as though any question they ever had about anything had been answered.

Hauser Pratt woke up drenched. He looked around, confused. Dreams had been outlawed. What memory he had of his life did not include the illegal images he had read about when he trained at the police academy. He thought of his wife, turned to look at her. Her silky blue nightgown stopped just above her knees. Somewhere in the night her blankets had been kicked to the side. Hauser stared at her round hips with a desire he felt might kill him. He reached over to touch her. She woke, grabbed his hand and pushed it away.

"What's wrong with you?"

He couldn't explain what he felt. He ran his hands along her legs.

Lucy sat up. "Are you insane? We don't have a conjugal appointment scheduled for at least another twenty days."

"I..,," he struggled. "I don't know what happened."

Lucy turned on the light in their bedroom. She scanned her husband quickly and saw what she suspected. "Your chip," she said.

He looked down. His identity chip had somehow unscrewed from the socket in his wrist. Patting around the bed, he found it near his pillow.

"Just put it back in." Lucy rolled over and covered herself with her blanket.

Hauser delivered the contracts to his boss and moved on to Identity Adjustment. How many times had he done this before? How many more jobs would he have to pull before he and his wife were moved into the White district? The lack of information about his past made it difficult for him to consider the future. Before he could think about it any further, his blue chip flashed and his mind went blank.

"Agent, ah, Pratt?" A man in a white coat, armed with a clipboard, extended his hand. "I'm Dr. Willowback. I'll be in charge of your reconfiguration."

Hauser shook the doctor's hand and followed him into the operating room.

Dr. Willowback pointed to a tilted chair in the middle. "Have a seat," he said. "We're still programming your Red chip."

As the doctor left, he turned on a music machine and the song everyone loved spilled out of a pair of speakers in the ceiling. Hauser sat down, leaned back and closed his eyes. He hummed along with the tune's repetitive lyrics, "*Don't think, don't think, don't think...*"

When the song finished, a DJ assaulted the speakers with his cheery voice—"K100! All music, all the time. That was `Don't Think,' the number one song since the revolution. Here it is again!" The infectious beat started up and Hauser, like anyone else tuned in to the station, sang along. "*Don't think, don't think,*" over and over and over.

45

Dr. Willowback returned with two other doctors. "Just relax," he said as he plunged a needle into Hauser's throat.

Lucy decided, as she did every day at twelve, to go to the town shopping center to purchase food for dinner and a pair of shoes or a dress, depending on what the other women were buying. She stood on the transit shuttle singing along with the song playing on the train's speakers, "Don't Think." The only example of music she had ever heard. She looked at the other women in her car. All were dressed in identical blue skirts, all carried the same blue, oval-shaped purse.

At the mall, she walked through the metal detectors, allowed a guard to thoroughly search her with his hands and then passed her wrist underneath a credit scanner.

"Blue chip," the machine announced. "Adequate level three credit."

"Level three, ma'am," the guard who frisked her said.

Of course, she thought, as long as my husband hesitates when his superiors give him work in the Red district, *of course* I'm just a level three. What's on level one? she wondered, are the colors of the shoes different? Her identity chip did not prevent her from thinking about life as a White consumer. When she tried to consider why she would be allowed to pursue that line of thought, however, her blue chip flashed and her mind went blank.

She followed a flock of women to the shoe store, where an instrumental version of "Don't Think" played on the loudspeakers. She scanned the rows of blue shoes. Had she purchased identical shoes yesterday? Looking at her feet, she saw the same exact shoes the store offered. Other women entered the establishment wearing blue shoes as well. They did not hesitate to take pairs of the same blue shoes off the shelves and examine them, trade them with the ones already on their feet, and parade in front of mirrors to see how the new versions of their old shoes looked.

Realizing she was making a scene by not shopping, Lucy walked over to a shelf with shoes in her size.

Hunter Polk darted through the alleys of the old world city. Buildings burned around him and the screams of other Reds being brutalized by corporate police filled his ears, urging him to find a safe place. Where? he wondered, where is safe? He looked at the flashing Red chip in his wrist. It blinked frantically, trying to make him forget what he had just thought. Only corporate authorities could remove it. What if I cut my hand off? he thought. The chip had been hooked into the veins in his wrist, he remembered. Trying to remove it would kill him.

He ran until he heard something lingering beneath the sounds of war. Different tones, played in a progressive succession. What should have been just noise struck him as beautiful. Beautiful? What does that even mean? He followed the sound to a rundown red-bricked building. Maybe it had been a school. Before the so-called revolution. Kicking in a glass window to the basement, he kneeled and poked his head through.

A small congregation of Reds huddled inside. In the far corner of the room, a boy tapped glasses with different amounts of water in each one with a spoon. The noise came from there.

"Hunter!" a younger woman shouted.

A man carrying himself as though he were in charge said, "Check him good."

Several men helped Hunter through the window. The man giving orders scrutinized his face, then lifted his shirt. Everyone in the room eased upon the sight of a scar down the right side of his body.

"What's the problem?" Hunter realized the noise coming from the glasses allowed him to think clearly. Despite the flashing Red chip in his wrist, his immediate memory remained intact.

The man in charge grunted. "You know damn well we can't trust anyone who's been gone as long as you have."

"How long have I been gone?"

"You've not listened to any proper music, have you?" The man in charge sighed.

Hunter thought about it. Music? It dawned on him that the noise coming from the glasses was music. Memories returned:

Music. The key to the revolution. When the brain followed a progressive melody, the identity chip could not short out its memory circuits.

The man in charge paced around Hunter. "Lorraine gave us the music box and then disappeared. It's possible she's been killed. The important question is: Do you have the tape?"

Hunter patted himself down. "I'm afraid not."

"Damn." The man in charge walked back to the front of the room. "Damn, damn and damn." The congregation stared at him, to which he quickly apologized. "I didn't mean to repeat myself. Old habit."

Hunter moved to the center of the room and sat down.

"You don't remember the tape, do you?" asked the man in charge.

Hunter considered lying, then thought better and shook his head. "Sorry."

"Not your fault." The man in charge took out a small box with a metal piece on the side. Turning the crank, he nodded towards the boy tapping the glasses of water. After the boy stopped clanging the glasses, the man in charge set the box on the ground. The most beautiful music of all danced from it in tiny, tin-like notes. "Beethoven," said the man in charge. "For Elise. From the old world."

A memory crept back into Hunter's mind. Beethoven. Ode to Joy. Lorraine... As the recollection of the woman he loved materialized, machine gun bullets swarmed through the room.

The congregation scattered as lead took out the glasses in the corner and the boy who played them. Hunter ran for the door, putting his hands behind his head. Before he made it through, the man in charge said, "Find the tape." He tossed him the music box.

Lucy Pratt sat on the couch, her legs propped up, waiting for her husband to return from work. She emulated the posture of a model on the cover of the magazine in her hands, *Modern Blue Chip Living*. It contained nothing but pictures of women just like her posing in different parts of their apartments which, of course, were identical to hers. Finding the magazine boring, which would ultimately trigger a shock from her chip, she quickly turned on the radio. "Don't Think" rumbled out of the speakers inside the walls of the apartment. She bobbed her head back and forth to the repetitive drum and bass line, singing along with the lyrics, *"Don't think, don't think, don't think..."*

Hauser Pratt came home at five, just as he did every other night. "What's for dinner?" he asked. Without waiting for an answer, he wandered to the kitchen and sat down.

Lucy noticed that her husband moved differently. How or why, she tried to fathom. Her chip wiped the thought away and she stood and walked to the kitchen. From the oven she produced two corporate dinners purchased, as far as she knew, earlier in the day. She put the food on the table and sat down across from Hauser.

"How's work?" she asked.

Hauser chewed on the rough meat provided by the corporate meal, spat out bone fragments and shrugged. "Usual."

"I bought some new shoes." She lifted her legs above the table to show him.

Hauser frowned. "They're wonderful, sweetheart."

Lucy felt she should say something, but knew it would only lead to a shock. Putting her foot down, she went to work on the food she knew—though never articulated—tasted terrible.

Hunter had been running all night. Searching through rubble, combing empty buildings, playing the music box the entire way to keep his Red chip confused. Where was the tape? And Lorraine? He remembered her now: Dark hair, green eyes, always focused, always *thinking*.

Exhausted, he set down in the basement of a war-torn public library to rest. The music box played as he fell asleep and recalled making love to Lorraine.

They were outside, where the corporate police could have caught them and executed them. She loved the danger and he loved making her happy any way possible. Smoke spilling out over the city turned the sky gray. Next to them, the music box played Beethoven. Their bodies moved with the Earth.

"Time can stop right now," he said between breathes, straining to invent words he thought romantic.

She smiled, wishing he would just shut up and work. Moaning, she grabbed him tighter and thrust her hips faster.

Covered in sweat, Lucy Pratt woke up. She looked around, confused. Where was she? She saw her husband in the dark. Felt the urge to touch him. "Hauser," she whispered, putting her hand on his belly, then tracing her fingers down.

Hauser woke, snapped on the light. "What's the matter?"

Lucy blushed. "I think," she said, "I think I'd like to have our conjugal appointment now."

Her husband ran his eyes up and down her body, as though he were examining a machine. He snapped his fingers and pointed at her wrist. "I thought maybe you had gone insane."

She realized what had happened and rummaged through the sheets. As she looked for her Blue chip she thought, Has this happened before? Yes, she realized, Hauser had lost his chip and asked for a conjugal appointment. Why?

Her husband found her chip on the floor, grabbed her wrist and screwed it back in.

As relief overtook her, Lucy forgot about the vivid images that interrupted her slumber. "Good night," she said to her husband.

They rolled onto their sides, facing away from each other, and fell safely back to sleep.

Lucy woke up at seven o'clock, stepped into the shower and washed herself. She put on a fresh blue skirt and blue shoes. She prepared a corporate breakfast and turned on the radio.

"Employees of the UCA, please stand for the Pledge of Allegiance."

Lucy stopped everything, put her hand over her heart and recited, "I pledge allegiance, to the seal, of the United Corporations of America, and to the profit margin, for which it stands, one company, under no regulations, with liberty and justice, to those who have earned it."

She went back to chewing on a rubbery, yellow imitation of eggs. The CEO of the UCA came over the speakers with his daily address:

"Good morning, employees. This is Prescott Heinz, your CEO. I am pleased to announce that we have made tremendous progress in the War on Poverty. I applaud the diligence of the Blue and White Chips, who have shopped with zeal while our allied corporate forces have worked around the clock to eradicate the Red menace. As you know, the War on Poverty will be a prolonged effort. It will take many, many years to achieve a solid victory. How many? Who knows. In the meantime, I ask that you consume our products and bear with us as we work to preserve our sacred way of business. Thank you and have a wonderful day at the malls."

ODE TO JOY

The CEO's voice was calm, reassuring, almost as gentle as the water in the clean machine. Lucy relaxed, finished her breakfast and prepared to go shopping.

Hunter ducked in and out of the shadows created by the half-destroyed churches and post offices and liquor stores and apartment buildings. Anytime he forgot who or where he was, he turned the crank on the music box and Beethoven brought him back to the present. *Like a compass*, he thought, *in time*.

A squad of corporate police had captured a dozen Reds, lined them up, and worked down the row shooting them in the backs of their heads. Hunter watched from behind the charred wall of a hollowed day-care center. His stomach turned as he saw poor people die, one by one.

When the police finished slaughtering their morning catch, they marched further down the street. Hunter raced from building to building, keeping an eye on the Blue Chip soldiers, occasionally running over dead bodies.

Then he saw someone he recognized. He turned the music box on, closed his eyes and thought. *The man in charge*. The one who had set him on task. Of course. The man in charge addressed a small group of Reds inside the remains of a super market.

Hunter ran over. "It's me," he said.

The man in charge did not seem to know him. Hunter wound up the box and watched as it first soothed and then revived the minds of his fellow Reds.

"Did you find the tape?" asked the man in charge.

Hunter shook his head.

"We'll never be able to sustain an attack without the music."

"It's OK," Hunter said. "I'll figure it out."

They sat quiet for a time, considering all their memories and how they might add up to a proper clue. Hunter recalled exactly what the plans had been:

He had found and, with the help of a mechanic named Walker (since murdered), restored an old transport, called a "car" before the so-called revolution. This "car" had a radio in it that could be manipulated so that a certain kind of recorded material could be played on it. In other words, the operator of the vehicle could actually *choose* what he or she listened to.

"The car is where I hid it, right?" he asked the man in charge.

"Only you would know that."

Of course, Hunter thought, on the edge of the city. Stalks of bark, once called trees, provided adequate cover for anything the *real* revolution needed to hide.

"Maybe the tape is still with the car," he finally said.

The man in charge shook his head. "You and Lorraine agreed to keep the two separate, in case one of you fell victim to a Time Shadow."

Time Shadows. The corporation's most sinister invention. A human being turned into a spy without being consciously aware of it. Any member of the revolution could be a Time Shadow and nobody, not even the Time Shadow itself, would know, as his or her identity would be programmed on his or her identity chip. Hunter looked at his wrist. Even he, he realized, might be a Time Shadow. Possibly the man in charge as well.

"We must move towards destroying the corporate police barracks, regardless of the risks," said the man in charge.

The barracks.

Hunter remembered the rest of the plan:

Roll the car as close to the barracks as possible and play the tape, which had forty minutes of Beethoven's Ninth Symphony on it. Long enough for a small army of Reds to dismantle and topple the corporate police presence in the old world.

"I think I should go to the car, see if that helps."

The man in charge narrowed his eyebrows.

"As far as I know, I am not a Time Shadow," said Hunter.

"That's what worries me."

The music box stopped.

The mall seemed packed. The CEO's speech must have invigorated the masses with consumer pride. It was their duty they, as well as Lucy Pratt, no doubt realized. And like her, they flocked to the shopping centers to do their part in the War on Poverty.

Lucy felt so patriotic she decided to buy a dress *and* a pair of shoes.

* * *

ODE TO JOY

Hunter found the car, buried beneath a pile of scorched trees. He moved enough of them out of the way to get to the door. Opening it, he grabbed his nose as the smell of industrial decay doused him.

Climbing inside, he looked around. What it must have been like, he wondered, to actually be able to transport yourself, long distances. In the middle of what he assumed to be the front of the car, a machine with a slot in it had been mounted.

"This must be it," he said. He looked at a wheel to the side of the radio, attached by a neck that had what appeared to be an old fashioned key in it. As he turned the key, a whining sound erupted from the area just in front of him. The engine, he remembered. It ran on a fuel that had vanished from the Earth just after the so-called revolution. Walker had managed to restore electricity to the car, but it would never move again by itself.

Lights inside the vehicle shined, including one on the radio. Hunter turned a knob on it and "Don't Think" crackled over the airwaves. Before it could drown the sound of the music box, he shut it off. The slot in it was empty. No tape.

Hunter got out of the car, buried it again with sticks and pieces of old tree trunks. He walked further, looking at the ground and the dead trees still standing.

In the distance, he saw a clearing. Tugged by familiarity, he moved towards the open land. Upon closer view, he realized he and Lorraine used to meet there. They put their bodies together without anyone's permission. He closed his eyes and recalled her arms holding onto him as they climbed, together, towards the most joyous memory he had.

And then they were separated. She, no doubt, caught by a Time Shadow. Executed. Or worse, recruited. Rumors suggested that the corporate police were capable of using plastic surgery and memory manipulation to change your best friend into a complete stranger.

Lucy Pratt sat on the couch waiting for her husband to come home from work. She turned on the television. The news anchor announced a special event would be broadcast that night. Hurry up, Lucy thought, I don't want to miss it!

Hauser arrived, glanced over his perfect apartment and sighed. "Dinner ready?"

Lucy led him to the kitchen. Prepared two corporate meals. "There's a special event on the television tonight."

Both ate in a hurry and then sat before the television with wide eyes. The live broadcast originated from a corporate stadium in another part of the new world. Two Reds were brought to the center of the venue, each armed with a metal instrument designed to gut and kill. Even though both prisoners were dressed in the same red clothes, had the same haircut, were of the same ethnic classification, Lucy felt sure she should hope for the one of the right side of the screen to win.

"I'm rooting for the Red on the left," her husband announced.

Lucy shook her head. Men, she thought, always wrong. Her blue chip erased her mind and she sat back as the competition on the news machine erupted.

The prisoners lashed at each other with their weapons. Flesh flew off in chunks and puddles of gore gathered around them. Within no time, both had severed limbs from each other and drawn enough blood that they ran out of energy, fell down and died.

An announcer proclaimed the match a "draw" and then promised more entertainment.

"I guess we were both right," Hauser said.

As Blue Chip janitors cleaned the bodies of the prisoners off the stadium floor, a man and woman dressed in nothing stepped in front of the screen and engaged in a conjugal appointment.

Lucy struggled with the thoughts rushing through her head as she watched the naked couple on the news machine. Her wrist flashed like a siren.

Hauser grabbed his head, covered his ears and said, "All right!" He got up, walked over to their communication machine and made a phone call.

Lucy tried turning her head from the television. She couldn't. Without facing her husband, she asked, "What are you doing?"

Hauser sat back down with a smile on his face. He shut the television off. "I've scheduled an emergency appointment," he said. "For consumer creation only, of course."

Lucy tried to hide her excitement. "Yes, yes. Consumer creation, of course."

ODE TO JOY

Kneeling in the open field, Hunter put the music box down, wound it up and let Beethoven retrieve his memories. He closed his eyes and saw Lorraine, naked. They had played the music box while their bodies were one. Afterwards, she explained to him about the song they had listened to in order to free their minds:

"Beethoven wrote the music, and some poet wrote the words," she said. She ran her hands through his hair in a manner mimicking the music itself. "The perfect union. They created the greatest piece of art ever known. That's why it's dangerous." She paused, kissed him, then continued. "So you and I have to separate now, until the time comes to attack. I'll take the tape, you hide the transport with the radio in it."

Lorraine dressed and ran towards the city with the cassette and the music box. It wasn't until after Hauser had hidden the car that...

He grabbed his heart. The corporate police had captured him, converted him. He wound the music box once more. The truth flooded his mind, made him dizzy. He was, in fact, a Time Shadow.

What had they promised him? he wondered. A White chip? In exchange for never putting his hands on Lorraine again?

Lorraine.

Picking up the music box and stuffing it inside his shirt, he ran towards the walls of the new world.

The lounge singer Marty Hopeless crooned a jazzy rendition of "Don't Think." The same chords, the same lyrics, over and over again. An example of 'diversity' in the new world. All couples listened to it when granted permission for a conjugal appointment.

Lucy undressed while Hauser did the same. Once naked, they kneeled on the bed and engaged in conjugal communication, pressing their lips against each other in a disciplined, ritualistic manner. Looking over her husband's body, Lucy felt certain there was something missing—a scar. How's that possible? Her wrist flashed and her mind blanked.

Hauser whispered, "I'm ready, how about you?"

Lucy glanced at her husband's consumer construction unit, saw that it stood in a creative stance. It didn't matter that *she* wasn't ready. She lay on her back and spread her legs. Clenched her eyes. As Hauser forced his unit inside her, she ground her teeth. He pushed and shoved in and out of her until her own creation unit

55

slicked enough to take his thrusting. It would be over soon, she realized, wondering why she had looked forward to it in the first place. And then another thought hit her:

This man has never been inside of me.

But they had had previous conjugal appointments, why else would she know what such an event...

Her Blue chip flashed and she began cheering her husband on—"Don't stop, don't stop, don't stop..."

Hauser emitted a growl, breathed deeply, and then rolled off of Lucy and collapsed onto his side of the bed. "Goodnight," he said, and fell asleep.

What noise actually woke her was unclear. The tin-like notes of an odd music she had never encountered, or the sound of her husband being beaten to death by a stranger.

Lucy sprang up in the night, turned on the light and saw a filthy Red caving her husband's skull in with his fists. She screamed and ran for the communication machine to call the corporate police. *It's true*, she thought, *the War on Poverty is absolutely necessary.*

Hunter pulled his bloodied hands from Hauser's dead body and chased Lucy down. He caught her feet just as she entered the living room. Both tumbled to the ground.

The helpless woman tried to scream again, but Hunter threw his weight on top of her, covered her mouth. He brought out the music box, wound it up, let it play.

Lucy's eyes widened. Such a brutal act had only been hinted at by the corporate news. *This can't be happening to me*, her mind protested. Then she realized the sound from the box allowed her to think. She breathed slower.

Hunter removed his hand from her mouth.

"Who are you?" she said.

"I'm in love with you," he said. "The corpse in the next room is *not* your husband. You feel nothing for him."

Thoughts, images, ideas, rushed into Lucy's mind. "What's happening to me?"

"You've been programmed by Identity Adjustment, by the corporation. You're a Red, like me."

"No way."

"Listen to me," he said. "They want me to find out where the tape is and hand it, and you, over to the corporate police."

Closing her eyes, Lucy thought about everything she had just witnessed. She saw Hunter's face, in the daylight, looking intense, but in a different way. She opened her eyes again. "Who am I?"

Hunter helped her to her feet and to the couch.

"Before they got us, reprogrammed us," he explained, "you were supposed to hide a cassette, a small piece of plastic you can store noise on, do you remember where you put it?"

The music box stopped. Hunter cranked it again.

Lorraine held her head in her hands, "I'm so confused."

"We have work to do," said Hunter. He traced his fingers along her shoulder, paid attention to the dip just before her neck.

She opened her eyes. "I remember." she said.

Lorraine led Hunter to a battered newsstand near the forest. Lifting the bruised and blackened shutters on the kiosk, she reached inside and pulled out a small plastic cassette. "Here it is," she said, and handed him the tape.

He looked it over. It certainly appeared as if it fit into the slot in the radio in the car. "Let's see if it still works."

She took his hand in hers and smiled.

They found the car and removed the camouflage.

Hunter opened the door and let Lorraine climb in first. He followed her inside, then turned the key by the wheel. He waited for the music box to finish playing the Beethoven piece, and then slid the tape into the radio.

"*Don't think, don't think, don't think...*"

The woman grabbed the music box from him and smashed it against the front of the car. "A White chip is worth more than anything you have to offer."

Hunter lunged for her and grabbed the music box. She tried to hit him but he caught her fist with his free hand and pushed her out of the car. Turning the engine off, he shook his head free of the cobwebs already being built by the corporate song, "Don't Think." He cranked the music box. Nothing happened. Shaking it, whispering to it, he realized the Time Shadow had done her job. Before he could wonder what the box in his hand was and why he needed to be concerned about it, the Red chip in his wrist flashed and he forgot everything he ever knew, other than the fact that the Blue and White Chips would find him, sooner or later, and compose his final thought.

"You game?"

Lucy Pratt sat across from the fat man, a corporate attack dog that would never climb into a higher credit bracket.

"How many more jobs before I get a White chip?"

Frank Boorhead laughed. "I'll bet you don't talk this way to your husband."

"How many more jobs?" She tilted her head. Impatience threatened to ignite her identity chip. *Hurry up*, she thought, *answer me!* But her wrist was already flashing.

Her boss chuckled again. He slid an envelope with a contract in it across the desk. "You start tomorrow." After a chomp on his cigar, he added, "Again."

What does that mean? Lucy thought.

Frank hummed "Don't Think" to himself, as though the woman wasn't even in the room.

Her Blue chip flashed and in less than a second, she wasn't.

(2004)

FRANKFURT STREET

Hello there, my little friend, what brings you out to the cold streets? I see, well, that is a mighty task for a youngster such as yourself. What's that? Why does that man look so? That is an excellent question and certainly bears the telling of the complete story. Are you in a hurry? No? Then sit on my lap and let me tell you about the ice cream man.

While you were still no doubt a toddler, resting quietly in a crib or perhaps your mother's arms, there once was a gentle man who sold ice cream to all the kids on Frankfurt Street. He drove his decorated truck up and down the lane. It played joyful music which attracted all the children. Sometimes the ice cream man would run out of ice cream, and so he would have to borrow one of the children to make a new batch.

What do I mean? Let me explain, and let us always remember, as is the moral of this and every other story you will ever hear in the New World, we cannot judge the ice cream man. Judgment is wrong, you know that, don't you? Very good.

Now, when the ice cream man was out of ice cream, he would take a child off the streets and put him in the back of his truck. They would take a merry trip to the ice cream man's house near the old forest. Inside this enchanted place was a machine that turned children into liquid.

You look frightened, my little friend, are you already making the horrific mistake of judging our friend the ice cream man? Judgment is bad.

By making children into liquid, what I mean is that the ice cream man would prop a child over a wood-chipper whose spout fed a machine that mixed human flesh and milk to create ice cream.

What did you say? Oh, no. My young companion, if I didn't know better, I would assume that you are judging our friend the ice cream man. I would hate to have to report a handsome young man like yourself to the Frankfurt Tribunal.

You haven't heard of that? Well, you have much to learn. All in good time.

It was customary for parents to object to the ice cream man's volunteering of their children for his services. One can agree the thought of never seeing your son again might cause sorrow. But most parents understood that it was for the good of the neighborhood that their child be sacrificed. And, as I cannot stress enough, judgment, on Frankfurt Street, is *absolutely* forbidden.

One parent, an evil man named Warren Knot, objected the day his son was called upon by the ice cream man. "If you take my boy," he promised the ice cream man, "I will kill you!"

As you can imagine, this outburst was not tolerated by the neighbors. The ice cream man, almost on the verge of tears, called upon a passing squad car filled with Corporate Police to settle the issue.

"This man is judging me," said the ice cream man, causing the entire neighborhood to gasp in shock.

"I will not allow my son to be violated and murdered by this monster!" shouted the reactionary father.

The CP's moved quickly on Mr. Knot and arrested him for committing an obvious and serious judgment crime. They comforted the ice cream man and helped Mr. Knot's son into the ice cream truck before taking Mr. Knot to the Frankfurt Tribunal.

Of course you don't know what the Frankfurt Tribunal is, you are too young and too smart. Only those who have committed a judgment crime have walked those dark halls. Warren Knot did so twice. The first time he was let off with a warning.

"Mr. Knot," the Presiding Voice, a woman dressed in ceremonial red, said in the sternest voice you would ever want to hear, "this court will not tolerate intolerance. Your exhibit today was inappropriate and has no place in an enlightened society such as ours."

"But, your honor," Warren pleaded, to which he was quickly interrupted:

"It is the opinion of this court that you spend one night in the stockades. You may then decide if you are with us, or against us." With that, the Presiding Voice clapped her hands and Warren was taken away.

Do you see that odd piece of wood just down the street? Very good. That is where the Frankfurt Tribunal sends big people who judge other big people. At least, the first time. As we shall see, the second time is not so forgiving.

What's that? Isn't the Tribunal making judgments as well? Young man! Do not question the manner with which we have created our society in the New World! Such an investigation will surely lead to judgment crime. By now you must realize that is the worst thing anyone can do.

Let us return to the story, however, of the, shall we say, unusual-looking man you now see stumbling around, asking for spare change. The ice cream man shredded Warren's son while Warren was in the stockades. Children enjoyed ice cream made from Warren's son the very next day. What was the son's name? Does it really matter?

What's that? You don't like it when I put my hand there? Are you judging me? I should hope not.

Yes, yes, the story. So Mr. Knot was released and he decided to follow the ice cream man to the enchanted house in the forest. Inside he found the blood of many volunteers all over the walls. The smell of rotting flesh and milk danced through his nose. But he was not there to admire the work of an artist, no, my little friend, he used his hands to beat the ice cream man to death.

Don't look so frightened. We cannot judge him for beating the ice cream man to death, no, that would be wrong also; When the CPs figured out who had murdered the ice cream man, Mr. Knot was taken before the Tribunal once more.

"Warren Knot," the Presiding Voice demanded, "can you explain your actions?"

Well, such a trickster was Mr. Knot that he produced tears and said, "He killed my son."

As you can imagine, the Tribunal came to the horrific conclusion that Warren's actions were the result of, yes, judgment. With a furious clapping of her hands, the Presiding Voice handed down Mr. Knot's Final Solution:

"Let his tongue touch his forehead so that he may forever think about the consequence of judgment."

And that, my little friend, is why that odd man walks in front of us with his tongue nailed to the bridge of his nose. But we mustn't think him too silly, otherwise he would surely make a case against us in the Tribunal.

What's that? Why, I thought you would never ask! Indeed, the magic house in the forest still exists. The machine no longer functions, but there are other fantastic things we can do there. Give me your hand and I will lead the way.

(2005)

EAST RIDGE

The school buses showed up overnight. Literally. Sunday they weren't there. Monday morning, they were. Traditional, yellow, unmarked. Jeremy Harper would have said nothing, had he not noticed there was one parked on each street between his nice, mundane cookie-cutter development house, and his insurance office in downtown East Ridge.

"You notice the school buses?" he asked co-workers.

Some of them had. Most hadn't. None showed concern.

"They don't have any writing on them," he said. "Isn't that strange?"

His co-workers said, "Sure." Then they'd say "So what?" or the equivalent.

"Why are they here? Why are they on every street?" he said.

They offered shrugs, empty-headed, stupid fluttering of eyelids. Most walked away, uninterested. He gave up on them. His job at Celestial Insurance amounted to nothing more than a McDonald's gig for college graduates—press buttons on a computer, save the company as much money as possible, and get a pat on the back in the form of a paycheck. His co-workers were former frat boys and sorority girls who'd somehow weaseled through geology or sports medicine majors and found their degrees next to useless.

Jeremy was there because he had a degree in philosophy and a minor in political science. An excellent recipe for unemployment or, worse, insurance. When he made perceptive jokes at work, his colleagues stared at him with blank faces. Sometimes they got angry at him for asking them to think about something other than money and reality television.

A fine example of the Celestial Insurance mindset occurred at a company picnic. There were competitions and prizes, most traditional—sack races, egg tosses, etc. One of the events was a joke-telling contest. Only Jeremy and another employee entered. When Jeremy explained to his boss his joke contained the word 'sex' in it, he was informed he would be fired if he told it. He withdrew from the competition. His co-worker asked the boss if a racist joke would be objectionable. "Of course not," said the big man. His co-worker then told a joke with a punch line arriving at the expense of all Asians, even the ones who worked at Celestial and were in attendance with their families.

So Jeremy took his concern home to his wife and two teenage boys. The buses were still parked on every street when he returned to his neighborhood. Just sitting there. No drivers, nobody claiming them. "This is it," he said to himself over a DJ on the radio complaining about the weather. "This is where they come and get us."

His house was in a suburb between East Ridge and Momo Creek. The zip code was officially Momo Creek, but nobody wanted to admit they were part of the blue-collar town. The residents of Quarry Road lived in nice, recently built white houses that all looked exactly the same. Two stories, three bedrooms, driveway on the left in front of a two-car garage.

Jeremy did his best not to consider the breadbox existence his life had taken. He had converted their garage into his private study and spent most of his time reading and rereading his favorite texts by Nietzsche, Kant and, Hume. That night, however, he confronted his family. First Wally and George, his pudgy sons who couldn't stop eating Suzy Q's and playing video games. "Hey fellas," he said.

They grunted, acknowledged they'd heard him, though they could not take their eyes off of the TV where they controlled two CGI soldiers in fatigues strolling an urban area and shooting anything that moved.

"Boys!"

His sons refused to turn around. Jeremy walked over to the television to turn it off. After a half a minute or so of trying to figure out how the modern marvel could be extinguished, he stepped in front of the screen.

"Dad!" said George.

"Turn the television off."

His boys looked at him with an expression suggesting he'd asked them to extinguish the sun.

"Turn the goddamn television off, now."

"What's wrong with you, dad?" Wally, the teenager of the two, asked.

"I want to talk to you guys."

"Not now, Dad!" George fidgeted on the couch like he had to go the bathroom.

Jeremy bit back the urge the slap them. That's what his father would have done. Then again, had that been a scenario involving his dad, it would never have gotten that far to begin with.

The boys looked past him to salvage their murder spree on the television.

Then it hit Jeremy. He felt around the television until he found the chord attaching it to the wall. He followed it to a power strip filled with plugs. Instead of pulling the one for the TV, he simply turned off the whole shebang.

The room went silent. His sons sat on the couch with stunned, wide eyes.

"Now you listen to me," he said. "I tell you to jump, you say 'how high?' Understand?" More of his father, a man he'd once called a "tyrant." His wife had convinced him not to govern the house the way his father had and, as a result, they had no control over their children.

"And if we refuse?" said Wally. He raised his chin, as though he actually believed he represented a threat of any kind.

Jeremy bit his lip. "Well, you just find out."

"That sounds like a threat, dad," said George. "Mrs. Connicker told us to report our parents if we think they're going to abuse us."

Jeremy tried not to laugh. The stupidity of modern American society, he realized, had infiltrated and poisoned the minds of his own children. He hadn't been paying attention and now his kids were over-emotional morons.

He forced himself between them on the couch and then put his arms, much to their disliking, around their shoulders.

"Boys," he said. "I'm your father. I would never do anything to hurt you. I simply wanted to ask you a question."

Wally let out a heavy sigh. The idea of having a conversation with his father was simply the greatest task anyone could have asked of him at that moment. Finally, he said, "All right, dad, what is it?"

"Did you boys notice the school buses on the streets today?"

"Where?"

"On the streets, on every street."

"You mean the buses taking us to school?"

"No, the ones parked at the end of the street. The ones that don't have any school district, or anything, written on the sides of them."

George shrugged.

Wally shook his head. "Sorry dad," he said. "I was texting my girlfriend on the ride to school today. I didn't see anything happening around me."

"Well," Jeremy said, attempting to extract critical thought from his children, "don't you think it's a little odd..."

"Odd?"

"Strange."

"Strange?"

"Weird."

"Weird?"

He took a moment. What word did young people use to denote things they didn't like? They were so afraid of being called a "hater," which was idiot-code for "having a different opinion," they'd limited their vocabulary. Then he remembered the word his daughter used to describe any male she found unattractive: "Creepy."

"Oh, creepy?" said Wally. "How so, Dad?"

"They're just sitting there, at the end of the street."

"Maybe someone parked them there."

"Good thinking, George, maybe someone parked them there."

"What's the big deal?" said George. "They're school buses."

"On every street?"

"There's kids on every street, Dad."

Jeremy paused, allowed his sons to catch up with logic. When it was clear they had not been taught how to think critically, he surrendered. "Never mind. I guess I'm just being silly."

"Crazy is more like it." Wally rolled his eyes and pulled himself off the couch. He walked over to the power strip and turned everything back on.

"Wally," said George, "crazy is a bad word. Our teacher told us it offends mentally challenged people."

"Where's your mom?" said Jeremy.

Susan Harper-West was busy heating three cans of ravioli in a pot on the stove. She blindly stirred the food while watching MSNBC on a small TV mounted on the kitchen wall. She barely noticed Jeremy when he walked in the room.

"Hey baby," she said, without looking at him.

"Susan," he said, "did you notice the school buses on the streets this morning?"

Obviously annoyed, she tore her attention away from Rachel Maddow and a panel of liberal arts professors agreeing with each other on how terrible racism had gotten in rural parts of America. "You mean the buses taking kids to school?"

"No, the ones parked at the end of the street. Every street. Unmarked, just sitting there."

"No, honey, I didn't." She returned her interest to the television.

"Isn't it a little weird?"

Susan fluttered her eyes. She made a clicking noise with her tongue and the top of her mouth to demonstrate how important Rachel's flogging of the working class was compared to her husband's concern.

"Jeremy," she said, "I'm watching Rachel." The tone in her voice suggested she was busy curing cancer and her foolish husband had interrupted her with a simple question about socks or beer or something equally unimportant.

"I'll be in my study." He walked out the side door leading to the garage.

Jeremy tried to ease his mind by reading his favorite passages from Henry Miller's *Tropic of Cancer*, a book he found more and more amusing as the women he knew insisted on calling it "misogynist." Eventually he fell asleep in his easy chair. He woke up around three in the morning. Initially, as he looked at the clock and saw what time it was, he was upset no one had called him in for dinner. Then he realized why he had been shaken from his sleep.

Outside, the steady pounding of helicopter blades disrupted the northern Illinois night sky.

"What the hell is going on?" He stood and shook his left leg, which was still asleep, and walked to the garage door to look out the window. He strained his head as close to the glass as possible. Just barely, he could make out the shapes of at least a dozen massive helicopters hovering over Momo Creek and East Ridge. He did the math in his head. The school buses, now the helicopters. All the paranoid fantasies he'd glanced over on the Internet while bored at work, all of them had warned of this. They called it the 'shadow government.' He'd dismissed the idea as paranoid fantasy. He put on his shoes and prepared to go outside to get a better look.

Sprinklers watered lawns up and down the street. "Who thought this was a good idea?" he said as he dodged water on the way to the sidewalk.

EAST RIDGE

The helicopters hovered in an almost perfect line across the sky. One every mile or so, by his calculations. He considered the chopper closest to his neighborhood. It was pitch black against the night sky. No markings, just like the school buses. A spotlight beamed from the bottom of the helicopter. It found him and stopped moving. He covered his eyes to protect them from the brightness. He jogged up the block to try to throw whoever was watching him. The spotlight followed him with unnerving precision. He ducked around the back of a house and crawled along a row of bushes. The light stayed right with him. Going back home would jeopardize his family, he realized. He turned and ran for East Ridge. The helicopter's beam tracked him until he ran out of its range. Before he could breathe easy, the spotlight from the next copter turned on and continued harassing him.

He ran all the way to downtown East Ridge. Whoever, or whatever, was watching him followed. As he made his way across 7th Street he remembered something from high school.

As a teenager, he'd had been part of a group of stoners called The Wastoids. They had several hiding places they went to during class to get high. One was a sewer drain by a park near Lake Jefferson. Inside the drain was a walkway that snaked underneath the entire town, all the way to Mount Zion, a large hill between East Ridge and Momo Creek.

He led the helicopter's tracking light straight to the park and then he climbed down and disappeared into the drain. The beam attempted to find him underground, but failed. He followed the path, by memory, to the opening right behind a church that sat by itself at the foot of Mount Zion. Cautiously, he stuck his head out and looked around. The helicopters appeared to be focused on downtown East Ridge. They splashed their searchlights across the rooftops and streets. Jeremy ran as fast as he could to the back of the old church. He broke a window and climbed inside.

"How ironic," he said to himself, "Momo Creek's only atheist, seeking salvation in a goddamn church."

The sun blasted through the tall stained-glass windows, heating up the church something fierce. Jeremy rubbed sleep from his eyes.

Preacher Red Ford and deputy Donny Purvis stood over him.

"Your the one that's always complaining about the pledge of allegiance," said Red.

It was true he'd tried, unsuccessfully to get the word 'God' removed from the pledge of allegiance in East Ridge's public schools. All three of them. He'd been shot down by the local court. Ultimately, he decided it wasn't worth the effort since he was the only one who recognized the Constitutional breach.

"Sure is," said the deputy. "Made himself a hell of a nuisance at my daughter's school."

"Officer, I'd like to press charges," said the preacher.

Jeremy was asked to stand while the deputy put handcuffs on him and then led him to his squad car outside the church. On the ride to the Momo County jail, he saw the buses were still there. The helicopters had disappeared.

"What's with the school buses?" he asked the deputy.

"The ones that takes the kids to school in the morning?"

"No," Jeremy said. "Those...the ones parked on the street." He used his forehead to tap against the window in the direction of one unmarked bus after the next.

Deputy Purvis barely looked over. "Not too concerned about it if it don't involve me or my family."

"Maybe it does."

"If that turns out to be the case, I'll deal with it then."

"You're not worried..."

"Mr. Harper, could you be quiet?"

EAST RIDGE

Jeremy sat back and watched Momo Creek roll by and then East Ridge. The buses were on every single street. No exceptions.

Momo County jail was part of a modest building that also housed the local court and police station. The prison, made up of three cells, was just beyond a wooden gate leading to the office area the city's half-dozen cops sat around until someone needed a cat pulled from a tree. On rare occasions, two or three officers would be dispatched to suggest, in the kindest way, to residents of Chicago who'd wandered into Momo County, to turn around and go back to the Windy City as quickly as possible. In the old days they used ropes and crosses and gasoline to do their encouraging. Now it just took a subtle patting of the automatic pistols in their holsters.

Jeremy was the only prisoner. He sat in the middle cell and listened to deputy Purvis and another officer, a younger guy named Kroger, talk about football:

"Who's going to QB the Bears this year?"

"Whoever it is, I guarantee you he'll be benched by the third game."

"Am I the only one that's sick of them relying on their defense?"

"Doubt it."

"I mean, really, historically, the Bears have always been a defensive power. But wouldn't it be nice, just one season, if we had a team that score a crap-load of points, just to help out the damn defense?"

"You read my mind, brother."

And so on. For hours. Statistics, stories about games from 1979 and 1985 and 1992. Words of praise for Mike Ditka. Words of intense hatred for Jim Harbaugh.

At noon, Susan arrived to bail him out. She was a lawyer and told the judge to release her husband on his own recognizance. On the car ride home, she gave him the business: "What in the name of Blue-Eyed Jesus were you doing breaking into churches?"

"I was hiding from helicopters."

She looked at him as long as she could without getting into an accident. "I missed a lunch with Stan Dillon, the assistant attorney general of Chicago. Do you know how important that meeting was?"

"Did you hear what I said?"

"Right, right. Helicopters." She shook her head in a manner suggesting a rodent had jumped on her face and that was the only way to get it off. "Helicopters..." She chewed on her lower lip. "Jeremy, when did you become a right wing lunatic?"

"Would you give me a little bit of credit?"

She looked at him very seriously. "You voted for Obama, right? Remember, we agreed we'd do our part to hoist Illinois out of the dark ages and elect someone other than a white man for once?"

"You know how I voted, dear. You filled in my absentee ballot."

"But, honey, unmarked helicopters, paranoia about school buses? That's the stuff rednecks worry about. Dumb, toothless, idiotic white trash rednecks. Because they're dumb, honey, understand?"

"Yes, of course, they're dumb and we're really smart. I forgot." He looked out the window as they passed one of the many school buses.

"What are we supposed to tell our children?" she said.

"The two zombies who don't even know my name?"

"That's not funny." She gave him another scolding glance. "They're young and impressionable. They see their dad is breaking the law, what do you think they're going to do when it comes time to make a decision between right and wrong?"

"I suspect they'll do whatever the television—their true parent—tells them to do."

Susan changed the topic: "I called your boss and explained what happened. He said to take the rest of the day off." Her voice lowered to her condescending, motherese tone. "You know they hate you as it is. One more rocking of the boat and you can bet you'll be looking for a new job."

"Yes, dear," he heard himself say. "I understand, dear," he said a few minutes later, though he hadn't heard what he was being chided for. She lectured him some more, though he'd stop listening beyond the pauses intended for his humble assurances she knew best.

He fell asleep in the garage again. Once more, he was nagged from his slumber by the pounding of the helicopter blades. The number had increased. There appeared to be enough to land on every street in Momo Creek and East Ridge.

He went into the main part of house and retrieved his wife's digital camera. He climbed the tiny, carpeted steps to the cramped second floor and then pulled down the stairs leading to the even tinier attic. A small, round window at the end faced the street. He pointed the camera outside and attempted to snap pictures of the helicopters. He would take a shot, review it, decide it was too dark to make out, and then repeat the process. He took twelve pictures before realizing the camera's lens was too slow to capture anything significant in the night sky.

The next day at work, no one spoke to him. They whispered when he walked by, nodded at him when they thought he wasn't looking. He was beyond "creepy." His stupid jokes about some guy named Aristotle walking into a bar with Thomas Jefferson and Aldous Huxley were the least of his obscene eccentricities. Now he was "one of those people," the kind who babbled on and on about birth certificates and Benghazi. He was "one of those people" who didn't understand the keys to happiness were large-screen televisions and cell phones with a thousand 'apps.' He wasn't hip to the crowd. He was a black sheep, a Judas Steer attempting to lead good folks down the sinful path of knowledge, straight to hell.

An asshole, as the former frat boys at Celestial Insurance had insisted all along.

He ignored them and took an assignment to snap accident photos on I-74, south of Rock Island. On the way out of town he snuck into a Best Value electronics store and purchased a video camera with night vision. It was the first time he had put down money on something "cutting edge," as far as technology was concerned, since he had reluctantly bought a CD player when he was in college.

As he drove down 74, surrounded by flat farmland freshly harvested, he perused the instruction manual for the camera. His thoughts on how he'd go about getting the best shots of the helicopters were gradually interrupted by activity on the side of the highway.

Men dressed in military fatigues with no national markings lined both sides of the highway. They were busy digging massive trenches. After a mile, Jeremy decided to pull over. Several soldiers looked up when he stopped his car. They glanced at each other and then went right back to gutting the land with shovels. "Hello," Jeremy said as he approached them. "How you fellas' doing?"

The soldiers acted as though he wasn't even there.

"Excuse me," he said, this time louder. "Just wondering what you guys are doing?" He didn't actually have to ask. One look down the line of them revealed a mile long trench, about the size of a mass grave.

"I said," he went to grab one of the soldiers.

The stranger swung his shovel up and threatened to bash his skull in.

Jeremy ducked and ran back to his car.

The soldier went right back to digging.

EAST RIDGE

Jeremy drove to the crash site he was supposed to photograph and then took side streets all the way back to East Ridge. He passed unmarked school buses the entire way.

He snuck out of his house at eleven. The helicopters had not arrived. Traffic was scarce. He drove into town, down 7th Street. No one noticed as he pulled over across the street from the park on Jefferson Lake.

He snuck into the park, to the opening in the sewer he had escaped into the first night he had noticed the helicopters. It had been sealed shut. He ducked through the shadows back to his car as quickly as possible. He drove, constantly looking over his shoulder, to Mount Zion. When he and Susan had been dating in college, they would go to the top and make out. The view was amazing. If the factories and steel mills in Rock Island weren't spitting out too much filth, you could see all of East Ridge and, on a particularly clear night, the pin-sized lights of Chicago.

He parked on the side of the road facing away from the town. He grabbed the camera and crouched in tall grass. He had to work from falling asleep. At one in the morning, the air from the south rumbled from the steady chatter of dozens of helicopters. There had to be fifty of them. As they flew overhead, Jeremy camouflaged himself in the grass. As soon as they were past him, he stuck his head out and watched as they landed, in the most mechanical, rehearsed fashion, on each street between Momo Creek and East Ridge. He turned on the camera and zoomed in to the nearest street.

Men dressed like soldiers carried machine guns as large as ten-year-old children. One by one, they kicked in the doors of Jeremy's neighbors and dragged them into the night and forced them on to the school buses at the end of their street. Some of the men, of course, protested. They were shot in the head, right in front of their families. The wives and children were convinced, at gunpoint, to hoist their dead fathers onto the school buses.

When every family had been put on the bus, the soldiers boarded. Jeremy assumed one drove and the others kept their guns trained on their passengers. The buses were driven in an orderly fashion out of town, toward I-74. They drove to the trenches. The families were led off and lined up, facing the ditches. Soldiers walked behind them and shot them in the backs of their heads. Jeremy's neighbors, his own wife and children, dropped into the mass grave.

Jeremy stayed hidden until the morning. When the helicopters and busses disappeared, all headed toward the east, he got in car and stepped on the gas, headed straight for Chicago. He searched the radio for a signal, for some explanation, someone outraged by what had happened. All he got was static. As the dirty highway signs announced he was getting closer to the Windy City, he felt, momentarily, relieved. Whatever had caused the holocaust in East Ridge couldn't possibly touch a massive clump of humanity like Chicago.

Before he knew it, he was on the Loop. Looking down at the Chitown neighborhoods, listening to Led Zeppelin on the radio. He caught something, however, in the corner of his eye. Something that nagged and disturbed his subconscious until he forced himself to look over.

On every street below, unmarked school buses had been parked. The people of Chicago, too smart, he figured, to be fooled the way his town had been, went on about their business. Not one person stood by any of the school buses demanding to know what they were doing there.

For Jeremy, the decision was easy. Drive to Canada and keep going until there was no more mass of humanity to be manipulated and slaughtered. People were stupid and there was absolutely nothing he could do about it.

(2008)

REJECTION

Chris Clark

He lounged on the roof of his apartment building in Koreatown, reading the latest issue of Arbogast Fantasy and Horror. None of the stories in it had been written by him. The first concerned vampires. It did nothing original but make for its setting a hockey camp in New Jersey. The next involved a serial killer. Following that, a five-thousand word cliché about alien abduction. Chris Clark read a page or two of each tale. When he got to the finale, a yawner about zombies feeding on a group of fishermen from Boston, he tossed the journal off the roof. It landed in the leaves of a palm tree.

"Good," he said. "Rats will use it to build a nest." He folded up his blue canvas chair and headed back into his apartment building.

As he made his way down the stairs and through the hallway, greeting his neighbors along the way (none of whom spoke English), he scrunched his lips to refrain from shouting. His past tantrums had drawn warnings from management. Upon receiving a rejection notice from Arbogast Fantasy and Horror, he usually threw his blue chair around his room, denting the walls.

The slips were always the same. Photocopied, standard memos. "Dear," it read, followed by a blank filled in with his name, handwritten. "We regret to inform you that we cannot use your story at this time." The magazine's editor, John Henry Francis, "signed" the note with a rubber stamp. He reminded Chris of the guard at the gates of Kafka's "Before the Law." He assumed, by John Henry's inability to publish anything remotely literary, that the guy had never read or even heard of Franz Josef Kafka.

He considered, at one time, sending John Henry Francis a copy of "In the Penal Colony" with a pseudonym in the by-line, certain the editor would be dumb enough to reject it.

Chris slammed the door to his apartment as he stepped inside. He removed his black shirt and black pants and threw them onto his bed. A desk wobbled on loose legs next to the bed, which took up half the space in the Bachelor's unit. Against the opposite wall stood a mini-fridge and a small table with a hotplate and blender on it. Pinned to a corkboard above his computer were rejection notices from Arbogast Fantasy and Horror. Fifteen. He had been collecting them for two years.

Lately, the span of time between sending a submission to Arbogast and receiving the rejection form had narrowed. In the beginning, three months passed before he received his self-addressed stamped envelope containing the bad news. His friend Gunter Fry, an older writer who lived in Santa Monica, had explained to him exactly what to look for the day John Henry Francis removed his head from his ass and accepted one of Chris's stories.

"They always send the contract right away," he said. "You won't get your SASE back. There'll be a big yellow envelope stuffed into your mailbox. Professional places like Arbogast, they send the check out with the contract. They want to take care of business as fast as possible. Snag those rights as soon as they can."

Gunter had been getting published since the mid-seventies. He fought in Vietnam and came home with some gruesome stories. Unlike Chris, he had the patience to write novels as well. Made just enough money to live by the ocean.

Chris went back to work on his latest story, "Something Terrible in the Darkness." He had gotten inspiration for it while waiting for the bus at Beverly Boulevard and Normandie. A walkway ran underneath the street, right next to a middle school. At one time students must have used the tunnel. Chain-link gates closed off the entrances on each corner. They were padlocked. A quick glance into the dim stairwell leading to the underground revealed the walls had been molested by graffiti. He asked himself, "Just what lurks down there in the pitch? Why aren't children allowed to go there anymore?"

And so he invented a new monster. Not a vampire. Not a werewolf. Not a zombie. A creature born from the concrete, from the brutality of the inner-city. A beast that fed on anyone foolish enough to look further into those tunnels.

He had been working on it for two weeks. His process was to write the first draft, let it sit for a few days, and then set to revising. After another draft or two, he hammered the story into a smooth read. Every writer he knew in Los Angeles had complimented him on just how tight his prose had gotten. Few of them approved of his subject matter. They were "literary" snobs. He argued that Kafka authored horror stories.

"At the very worst," they responded, "Kafka might have been dabbling in 'magical realism.'"

Chris fine-tuned the seventh draft of "Something Terrible in the Darkness" and printed it out. He wrote a standard cover letter detailing his publication credits, attached a SASE and stuffed it all into a giant, yellow envelope.

Mailing a piece to Arbogast had become a ritual as well. He walked to the Sanford Station post office on Sixth Street and Harvard. A line of people packed the lobby in a half-circle. While there were six windows for service, there were never more than two employees on duty at any time.

He waited twenty minutes to step up to a window. The clerk behind it, an elderly woman with thin hair, dyed red, identified by a crooked name tag as 'Roberta,' seemed to be competing with a snail somewhere, seeing if she could move half as fast. Since Chris didn't have to teach that day, he didn't mind the two minutes it took her to weigh the envelope and put a stamp on it.

Her fingers moved in slow-motion as she typed the weight into her computer and, even slower, turned and said, "Dollar seventy-eight."

Chris paid her, thanked her, and went back home to write a new story.

Five days after mailing "Something Terrible in the Darkness," his SASE sat in his mailbox. His own handwriting grinned at him. "What the hell?" A Korean family got off the elevator the moment he shouted. As they passed him, the father shook his head.

Chris put his hands and the fresh rejection letter in his pockets. He squeezed down on his thighs to remind himself not to get angry in public. Instead of returning to his apartment, he headed for the bus stop at Normandie and Third.

"That sonofabitch," he said. "Five days? Are you kidding me? That piece of crap didn't even read the story!"

He got on the Line 206, headed north to Santa Monica Boulevard where he caught the express bus to the west side. Rush hour. Every seat was occupied, forcing him to stand, holding on to the bar overhead while containing his rage. It took ninety minutes to cross town. As soon as he saw the horizon vanish over the ocean and the generic roller-coaster and ferris wheel on the pier, he relaxed. He got off at Santa Monica's version of Third Street and hustled over to Montana Avenue. Gunter lived down the road from the Aero theater. That was where and how they had met. The Aero had been running a series of horror movies. One of them, The Hollywood Cocaine Massacre, had been based on a book by Gunter and he had been invited to speak before the screening. In classic Gunter Fry fashion, he badmouthed the film and Hollywood and then showed the audience both of his middle fingers before storming out of the building.

REJECTION

Chris had followed him, awestruck by his audacity. "I got to buy you a drink," he said. Gunter, being, like most writers, unable to turn down such an offer, agreed. He took him on as an apprentice of sorts, telling him what to read and where to submit his stories.

As he made his way down the palm tree-lined street, he saw that Gunter's car, a rusted, brown 1957 Chevy, sat in his small driveway next to his yellow, stucco house. Battling knee-high grass, he trudged across the front lawn and knocked. He waited and beat on the door again, louder.

Gunter Fry ripped it open. A short man, maybe five-two, his eyes were dark, wild marbles racing up and down and side to side, barely contained behind giant, square glasses. "Chris Clark," he said. "'The hell brings you to Santa Monica?"

"I need to know the secret."

"Kid," he said, "there's no secret. How many times have I told you?"

"You and I know that's bullshit." He moved forward, insisting Gunter let him in. "The hacks are published while the Philip K. Dick's starve."

Gunter stepped aside. "You better not be calling me a hack, kid. I'll crack your larynx with the palm of my hand."

Chris paced between a glass display case holding Hugo awards Gunter had won and a neon-orange couch that might have been fashionable in 1977. "That's just it," he said. "You're one of the only great writers being published today. There has to be a secret."

"Ever read any of my work?" Gunter asked.

Chris looked away. "Of course."

Gunter laughed. "I know for a fact that you haven't."

"I read Disgruntled Gumdrops. You don't believe me, go ahead and quiz me."

"But you never read any of the first stories I published."

"How do you know?"

"Trust me," he said. "You wouldn't want to."

"I'm sure they're awesome." Chris paced faster. "I have to know what the trick is, how to get past the dragon at the gates."

"Kid," Gunter said, "I'm having dinner with Mary's sister and brother-in-law at six. I've got to get ready." He nodded towards a shot glass and bottle of whiskey on a coffee table by the couch.

"Just tell me what I need to do to get that jackass at Arbogast to consider my work."

Gunter looked at his watch. "All right," he said. "I'm going to give you something. You didn't get it from me. Only use it on John Henry Francis. He's the only one who deserves it."

The old writer disappeared into his den and returned after a minute with a jug made out of blue, pharmacist glass. Inside sloshed a molasses-like substance. He crossed the room and went into the kitchen. He came back with a Tupperware box big enough to hold a couple of sandwiches. After opening the jug, he filled the plastic container with some of the dark liquid.

"What's that?"

"Ink." The expression on his face resembled the one he wore just before giving the audience at the Aero the middle finger.

"I have ink."

"Not like this." He finished filling the container. He corked the jug and put the lid on the Tupperware. After handing the plastic box to Chris, he said, "Put that in your printer when you're ready to print the next story you send to Arbogast."

"Is it going to make the words look prettier?"

Gunter grunted. He put the jug on the table by the couch, next to the whiskey. "You must not let the ink touch your hands. When the story is printed, put it directly in the envelope, seal it, and send it off. Even when the ink is on paper, you must not let it get into your skin."

John Henry Francis

Lunch stank. The people from Punting Press were hippies disguised as executives. They came to the meeting dressed in jeans and cheap, K-Mart button-down shirts. The big cheese, Katie Prudent, had sported a flimsy summer dress that showed her form whenever she stood in front of the sun-drenched window.

John Henry Francis looked at himself in the mirror while washing his hands in the restaurant's bathroom. He had spent twenty minutes that morning getting his hair to spike. Who did these people think they were talking to? His serious-gray Armani suit should have told them who ran the show. His Guess shoes went for five hundred bucks a pair. And they had the nerve to give him the shrug.

"Well, Mr. Francis," said Katie, "we'll read the stories and if everyone can come to a positive consensus, we'll take the next step."

Give me a break, he thought. What else is there to do? Space Conflicts, the 2002 Hugo award-winning collection of Star Wars rip-offs had been his baby. He wouldn't have set up the meeting if he didn't think the anthology would sell. He wanted to shout at them, "I'm in charge of Arbogast, understand? My magazine is in every airport from here to Butt-knuckle, Washington. Has anyone even heard of Punting Press?"

He dried his hands. The hippies caught a cab as soon as they paid the bill. At least they had done that much for him. He hated Japanese food and he hated, even more, leaving midtown. Checking his suit to make sure everything looked straight, that his shoulders were tugged tight to accentuate the work he had done that morning at the gym, he blew his reflection a smooch and strutted out.

A stack of manuscripts had been loaded onto his desk. When he started at Arbogast, there had been a team of readers. Once he got the position of editor, he puckered up and kissed the publisher's ass by suggesting the company save money and let the assistants go. "I know what sells," he assured his bosses.

Their interest in profit trumped their taste in literature.

John Henry Francis took his coat off and folded it over a green, vinyl chair in the corner of his office. He sat at his desk and got to work. The first envelope he opened contained a Tolkienesque mess from somebody in Kansas. Giving it a courteous half page skim, he decided no such thing as a writer from Kansas existed. The hayseed who had scribbled the troll and hobbit tripe hadn't even included a self-addressed stamped envelope. He tossed the whole thing into his round, industrial steel garbage can.

The next submission: A werewolf yarn written by someone from Boston. The writing stank but the story broke no rules. "I like it," he said. He hadn't read much of it, just enough to know it mimicked what Arbogast had been publishing since he had become editor.

He prepared three envelopes with rejection memos, each going out to various states in the middle of the country. "Why don't you guys just stick to farming and working in factories?"

Then he saw a familiar return address. "When is this loser going to get the message?"

Chris Clark. Some artsy-fartsy writer who lived in Los Angeles. Normally, John Henry didn't mind reading anything from the west coast, as long as it adhered to the standards of the magazine. But this Clark guy, he blended genres and did things nobody who consumed horror or science fiction had seen before.

John Henry had read letters sent to Weird Tales back when they made the mistake of printing stories by H.P.

REJECTION

Lovecraft. The subscribers hated them. They were the equivalent of a fat kid whose parents had enough money and gall to send their little tugboat to a finishing school. Certain things just didn't belong in the mainstream.

Chris Clark presented a shining example. The pompous jerk probably referred to his scribbling as "postmodernism," or some other pompous term the sandal-wearing flakes at universities called their radical ramblings in effort to justify their refusal to be normal. The last time he had gotten one of Clark's submissions he had thrown it away without even looking at it.

Feeling charitable, John Henry told himself his conscience would reward him if he gave Chris Clark the same consideration he gave all the arrogant turds who tried new things. He opened the envelope and pulled out the contents. It contained the usual cover letter, detailing Clark's worthless publication credits. Who had ever heard of The Magnolia Review? Some college rag you found on campuses and one or two bookstores that stocked literary journals to silence anyone who bashed them for selling dependable John Grisham and Dean Koontz novels.

He set the cover letter aside and began reading the story, "Ink and Mirrors." More attempts to be clever in a world that didn't pay a penny for original ideas. John Henry let his eyes scan the first few paragraphs. When he felt he had read enough, he reached for the pile of pre-printed rejection letters.

And then he stopped.

For some reason, whatever he had read, it caused a reaction similar to that of tearing down the first hill of the Cyclone, over at Coney Island. He wanted to finish it. As he read on, he recognized the writing as stream-of-conscious. In his mind, he calculated how someone would market it—"It's like Henry Miller meets Harlan Ellison. All the furious attitude of the id, right there on the page."

He shook his head. "What the hell am I talking about?" Publishing it would scar Arbogast's reputation. Once more, he tried to put a rejection letter in the self-addressed stamped envelope.

Something stopped him. I've got to read it all, he thought. Blood rushed through his body, like he had been seasoned, like a twelve-year-old boy finding a stash of Playboy magazines in his father's work shed. His heart beat faster. Putting the story in front of his face again, he lost himself in the words, caressed the ink on the page with his fingertips.

The prose looped together like music, like a Charlie Parker solo, flying crazy in and around a melody in a way that should not have worked. Like Dali meets Picasso. James Joyce meets William Burroughs. Nonsense. Beautiful.

"Chris Clark," he said when he finished, "congratulations." He dropped the story in the wire-meshed acceptance basket on a small table next to his desk. His body continued to tingle with excitement, like the first time a girl had put her hands in his lap. He ignored the sensation and reached for the next submission.

It had been sent from Dubuque, Iowa. Normally, he would have grabbed the SASE, stuffed it with a rejection slip, and moved on until he found a submission from one of the coasts. Instead, he took the manuscript out and read it.

Nothing more than a vampire tale set in Chicago. Maybe I'm learning a lesson, he thought. A thousand words in, he noticed the light hitting the page flickered. Craning his head to see if the fluorescent overhead needed to be replaced, he saw that the long tubes were pulsating blue and white.

"What the hell?"

He cleared the envelopes out of the way and stepped onto his car-sized, mahogany desk. His Guess shoes failed to grasp the slick surface. He worked to get a footing and then reached for the housing on the light and tapped it. Sprinkles, like tiny stars, floated down each time he hit the lamp.

Perhaps, he thought, I'm having a panic attack. His mother had had them when she went through menopause. She compared it to stumbling into pockets of insanity. He jumped down off of the desk.

"Just keep reading," he said. He picked the vampire story back up and forced himself to focus on the words. It worked for a moment, and then the sentences melted and bled together. When he held the page away to look at it from a distance, it became an inkblot test, reminding him of all the shrinks his mother had taken him to when he was a child in effort to prove him a genius. She could never find a doctor who would diagnose her son as anything beyond ordinary.

His heart thundered like a drum beaten by a maniac. The far wall of the office bubbled like boiling liquid. "Someone slipped me something at the restaurant," he said. "Evil hippies!" He struggled for the door. The floor waved like an ocean. Air whipped like a violent wind in and out of his ears. He forgot why he had crossed the room.

Then, for just a second, he forgot who he was.

The police, he thought, I'll call the police. I'll have an ambulance take me to the hospital. They have to have something there that will make this go away. He grabbed the phone and put it to his ear. The dial tone wailed like a bomb siren. The chord twisted and turned. It became a snake, crawling up his arm to strangle him. He threw the receiver at the desk.

The walls closed in, threatened to squish him. Natural light blasted through the window. The only escape, he realized.

Climbing onto his desk once more, John Henry took three steps and launched himself through the cheap glass his cheap bosses had installed to save money on air-conditioning. He flew over Madison Avenue and tumbled to the Earth, trying to grab onto ladders and ledges his mind convinced him existed just before his entire body spread across the concrete like a glob of jelly.

Gunter Fry

Two rows of his bookshelves were filled with contributor copies he had received from Arbogast and other fantasy magazines over the years. Their spines were perfect. Most of them had never been opened. He admired them every day just after he finished writing his mandatory two-thousand words. Those stories had built his career.

The jug of ink still sat on his writing desk. He remembered picking it up in Thailand. He had been an officer in the war. His job: Dispatch troops into the jungle to ward off the Viet Cong. Then, he and the other officers would take a helicopter into Saigon or Malaysia or Thailand. They'd trade cigarettes for whores and consume any drug or alcohol they could find.

Outside a temple in Bangkok, he had met a homeless man who claimed to be from Siberia. He spoke perfect English. Gunter told him he wrote stories and the man traded him the ink for a pack of Lucky Strikes.

He didn't believe him at first. Two years after returning to the states, a brutal period in his life when nobody would publish his work, he tried it. Every manuscript he sent out got accepted after that, including his first novel. Once his name had been established, he no longer needed the ink.

These things ran through his mind as Chris Clark showed up, grinning. Gunter had never seen the kid smile.

"Look at this," said Chris, waving a large, yellow envelope with the Arbogast insignia on the return address. He opened it and pulled out the contract with a check for three hundred dollars stapled to it.

REJECTION

"Congratulations, kid." Gunter let him inside his house. "Guess this calls for a toast."

They climbed the narrow staircase leading to the second floor. At the far end of the hallway, a screen door led to a balcony. From there, they could drink and watch the ocean.

"I assume you used the ink," Gunter said after they sipped from their glasses.

"I'll give you one of the contributor copies when it gets printed."

Gunter almost choked. He waved his hand before he could speak. "Listen, kid," he said, "never read anything that got published because you used the ink."

Chris frowned.

"I know you want to see your work laid out professionally." He set his glass down. "The thing is, the ink is only half the magic. Combined with the words, the story itself becomes a drug."

Chris shook his head. "That's absurd."

"Anyone who reads your story now will go mad." He paused, made sure he had the kid's complete attention. Then he said, "Even you."

(2008)

Before the Internet revolution in publishing, Stanley Rutgers was crafting radical narratives mainstream publications wouldn't go near in the early 2000s. His work eventually found a home with online and on-demand publications in the early part of the following decade. His based narratives pre-date the #PulpRev movement that restored traditional pulp fiction in the literary eco-system. Rutgers was found dead in his home in 2019. While the official cause of death was suicide by a self-inflicted gunshot wound, no accounting has been made for the fact that no less than three entry wounds in the back of Rutgers's skull were noted by the initial coroner responsible for the autopsy. Amongst underground conspiracy theorists, it is taken as fact that Rutgers was murdered.

Rutgers is survived by his wife Mary and three daughters.

Enjoy the following excerpt from Ronin Heck's
SAME SONG, DIFFERENT BEAT

Chapter One:

The radio on the transport should have been louder. Teo Paz could still hear the ringing. Normally, the high-pitched hum vibrating behind his left ear vanished the moment any form of popular entertainment occupied his thoughts. The DJ introduced the song as Suzanne Minassian's latest version of "Sunshine Manifesto." The DJ claimed the beat had been modified. Suzanne's vocal had not been altered. Teo found it impossible to determine whether any aspect of the song had changed since it usually played at volumes quelling the chance for conversation with his fellow workers on the bus.

He stared out the window, hoped the scenery might distract him from the ringing. The bus turned onto Van Ness and rolled past the district garbage heap, a mountain of trash sitting on the old Hollywood Forever cemetery. Level one workers climbed the peak's spiral foot path with sturdy hemp bags strapped to their backs. They scoured the refuse for anything eligible for the recycling plant. Some had been tasked with removing coveralls from expired workers. They constantly wiped their noses, presumably to combat the stench of rot and decay. It reminded Teo how lucky he'd been to move into level three on account of his veteran status. He'd worked the garbage hill briefly, right after the war. He'd sloshed over moist, empty boxes of food and human and animal remains, day after day. Any time the smell of death compelled him to complain, he'd stare past the trash, at the abandoned buildings in downtown L.A. and the smokestacks and factories just beyond. He'd considered his job superior in that he spent his time on the clock outdoors, breathing what remained of the world's natural air. His positive attitude paid off. Inspectors eventually recommended him for advancement to a higher level.

The transport arrived at Mutual Foods Northwest five minutes before Teo's shift started. He filed off the bus with several colleagues. They waited by the doors for Kang Ji Young, their manager, to let them in. The morning sun bulled through dirty, bloated clouds blanketing South California. Teo tugged at the collar on his coverall. He'd worn his red version. The day before he'd come to work in his blue version. He had a different color for each day of the week. The Mutual Organization referred to this as diversity. The clip on his ID badge dug through the thinning fabric and into his skin. He adjusted it, noted the stark, orange L3 underneath his name, how much nicer it looked than an L1 badge. His hairline in his photograph on the badge reflected how much time had passed since he'd been promoted. The red coverall, apparently, would not hold up much longer. He'd have to buy a new one. Another expense. He tried to hide his disappointment. Like most of the men he knew, he wanted to save his credits for a Cheetah 3000, a sports car Buster Minassian advertised on television every night. The sleek, two-door automobile zipped across ancient highways in other regions. The night before, for instance, Buster had screeched to a halt in front of the ruins of Mount Rushmore. No matter how much Teo tried, however, he couldn't escape nagging bills and personal needs holding his credit balance hostage, stagnant.

And the sun, goodness, did it burn. He preferred not to sweat before stacking boxes on shelves in the market. His face must have revealed his displeasure. Makiko Hana, a young woman who worked in the dessert aisle, approached, her normally pleasant smile strained. She'd worn her purple coverall and painted her eyelids a matching color. "How about this weather?" she said to Teo.

"It's wonderful," he said.

"It is. It is wonderful. Amazing. Amazing and wonderful, yes?" She brushed her shoulder length hair behind her ears. Sweat had formed near her temples. Surely, she didn't enjoy the heat, either.

"Indeed," said Teo. "Wonderful. And amazing." He laughed. "Can we go so far as to say it's wonderfully amazing?"

She played with her hair again. Flirting? She must not have known his situation, how he'd been sterilized after the war, had been barred from procreational privileges. "Did you watch *The Minassians* last night?"

"Yes, yes I did." He didn't have a choice. The ringing in his ear would have driven him insane if not for the television in his apartment. "I like how they got a new actress to play Trudy Minassian."

"Oh, yes!" Makiko's eyes rolled. Her thin lips relaxed. "So, so wonderful. So creative. So amazing."

"Well," said Teo, "you knew one of the daughters would be replaced this week. They spent last week shuffling the parent characters around so much, it only made sense."

"I know, I know," said Makiko. "Trudy has my favorite dialogue, so, you know, it made me really happy to see the producers use her to make the show different."

Teo preferred the previous Trudy. In spite of his sterility, he had desires. He couldn't discuss them. Certainly couldn't act on them. Since the storyline of the television show never changed, he'd lost interest in its dramatic aspects. He fantasized, instead, of making love to one of the many Minassian sisters. Another distraction from the ringing in his ear.

Ji Young unlocked the doors. The staff entered the building in an orderly manner. One by one, they greeted the supervisor:

"Good morning."

"It is a good morning." She'd worn a majestic white, gold-trimmed coverall. The variety of color demonstrated what the writing on her badge confirmed: L5 (though she'd once been a level seven). It also matched the golden earrings she'd worn in the photograph on her badge. She'd wrapped her straight, black hair into a bunch with strands poking out and bobbing anytime she moved her head. "A wonderful, amazing morning, yes?"

"Yes," her employees responded. "A wonderful, wonderful, amazing morning."

When Teo greeted his boss, he could not make eye contact with her. He and Ji Young had an embarrassing history from which he'd never recovered. She'd been decent enough not to discuss it with anyone. Not with the staff and, most importantly, not with any inspectors from the Mutual Organization. Frankly, she should have been grateful *he* hadn't reported *her*. Three years older than him, she had, one day, suggested they engage in unsanctioned procreational activities. She said she'd been rendered infertile by the Mutual Organization. A penalty endured once demoted to a lower level. No one would ever find out. The idea appealed to him. He'd been attracted to his boss since he'd been assigned to her store. But when it came time to engage in the act, he remembered the Mutual physicians assuring him that part of his body no longer functioned for purposes pleasurable or constructive. His body responded, retreated. His boss did her best not to chastise him, make him feel less useful than other men. But she'd also been cold to him forever after. The thrilling tint of unspoken attraction decorating their conversations disappeared.

She greeted him without looking at him and moved on to the next worker in line. Oh well. The last thing anybody wanted? Complaint. He followed his colleague Miguel Pacheco to the stockroom to swipe his ID badge and get to work. Miguel patted him on his shoulder. "You see the new version of the commercial for the Panther 3000 last night?"

"You mean the Cheetah 3000?" he said.

Miguel squeezed the bridge of his nose and closed his eyes. "Pretty sure it's called a Panther, my friend." He shook his head and pinched the ends of a thin mustache he'd recently decided to grow.

Jabbing him with his elbow, Teo said, "No reason to dwell on it. Someday, we will all have the car of our dreams. Just need to keep working." He swiped his ID badge and pulled a shopping cart from a row near the back door. He pushed it around the corner to the stockroom. The front wheels squeaked and wobbled. He read the morning instructions on a clipboard hanging on a hook on the end of the first aisle of vegetable powder. The order called for amber boxes. He loaded his cart with as many as possible and struggled to push it to the vegetable section.

He shoved the remaining flaxen boxes from the day before to the end of the shelf and replaced them with amber boxes. Ji Young turned on the overhead speakers and "Sunshine Manifesto" filled Teo's ears with an electronic, mono-rhythmic beat and a woman's voice singing, "Wonderful, Amazing," over and over again. As Teo continued shelving vegetable powder, the song faded out. A Mutual DJ announced, "Amazing, wonderful! Here's the same song with a different beat." The anthem repeated. Teo couldn't be certain, but it seemed the beats between the two versions of the song had not changed at all. It seemed, in fact, *nothing* had changed. He began to suspect the vocalist had been the same woman singing the song since it had first been produced, just after the war. If he mentioned it, said so out loud, would it be considered a complaint?

As customers filed in, Teo kept the vegetable aisle stocked. A solid wall of amber. The moment a customer grabbed a box, Teo replaced it. He stood on guard, between the stockroom and the vegetable aisle. This represented the amount of authority and responsibility he'd been granted and it constituted the most fulfilling part of his life. On this day, however, he couldn't shake the concern that "Sunshine Manifesto" had been the same song, set to the same beat, since it had become the only legal music in South California. When Ji Young closed the store for a lunch break, Teo decided he had to say something.

In the break room, he sat next to Miguel. As they stirred meat and vegetable powder into a bowl of steaming water, Teo said, in a voice intended for Miguel and no one else, "Have you ever listened to 'Sunshine Manifesto' closely? I mean, really, *really* closely?"

Miguel shrugged. "It's a wonderful song. Amazing." He lifted his spoon to his nose to give the food a whiff.

"And the many different versions," said Teo, "are they really different?"

"My friend…" Miguel put his spoon back in his bowl. "Why would you even ask such a question?"

"A joke," said Teo. "I was joking." He looked around. Makiko Hana had stopped stirring her powder. She stared at him with the concern she'd worn earlier, when she suspected he hadn't enjoyed waiting outside, in the heat. "I wasn't serious," he said. Same explanation, different words. Did she buy it? Would she forget all she'd seen that day?

Following lunch, Ji Young led the staff on a forty-five-minute walk in a circle around the building. The Mutual Organization referred to this as recess. This allowed the workers to simultaneously digest their food and exercise.

SAME SONG, DIFFERENT BEAT (Sample Chapter)

Then the market reopened and Teo resumed stocking shelves in the vegetable aisle. More customers showed up as factories and recycling plants let out. People in coveralls much more stained and abused than Teo's or his colleagues' purchased boxes of vegetable and meat powder. Some splurged, apparently not saving for a car or any other luxury item, and bought dessert mixes. Must have been nice. Teo supposed if one had resigned to life in a lower level, why bother attempting to save for something like a Cheetah 3000? Did that qualify as a judgment? He'd have to keep his opinion to himself.

Near closing time, an inspector visited the store. Inspectors walked the aisles, made sure the boxes of food were arranged in an orderly manner. The inspectors would chat with Ji Young. Sometimes they'd strike up conversations with workers. It usually went something like this:

"How's your day been?"

"Amazing. Wonderful. Couldn't ask for more."

"That is amazing. And wonderful. Carry on."

On that day, however, the inspector must have spoken with Makiko. Teo didn't hear the conversation. He'd been focusing on the song playing on the speakers. The monotonous beat drove him up and down the aisle, filling gaps on the shelves with fresh boxes of vegetable powder. The inspector rounded the corner from the dairy aisle and asked to speak with him. No formal greeting, no questions about how things were going. The inspector said, "Teo Paz? Let's step into the break room for a moment." At that point, Teo understood someone had voiced concern. Makiko, he assumed, though his conscience suggested he jump to no conclusions.

The inspector offered him a place at the lunch table. He sat opposite him, allowing Teo to read his ID badge: Claude Ramirez. Had he ever seen this inspector before? So many of them looked alike. They wore gray, lifeless coveralls. Same attitude, different names. Claude Ramirez said, "I understand you've been questioning the authenticity of the latest rendition of 'Sunshine Manifesto.'"

Teo shook his head. "No, no." How honest should he be? He didn't remember much of the war, but he did recall the whole thing being fought over certain people, people he agreed with, insisting their opponents had no integrity. They couldn't be trusted. They told lies. They'd lied about history. They'd lied about contemporary society. They'd lied about the future. He said, "I can't really tell if the beat is different. You know, from one version to the next."

Claude Ramirez relaxed his shoulders. He leaned back in his chair and folded his hands across his chest. "Mr. Paz, have you counted the beats per minute?"

Teo admitted he had not.

"Let me give you an example," said Claude Ramirez. "Do you remember last week's version? The previous Trudy Minassian sang it. That version had one hundred and twenty beats per minute. The new version, Suzanne Minassian's version, has one hundred and twenty-*two* beats per minute. I'd be happy to take you to the studio it was manufactured in and have an engineer demonstrate the difference."

Goodness. Teo admonished himself for having spoken up in the first place. "I'll take your word for it."

This seemed to please Claude Ramirez. He smiled and bobbed his head. "Good, good." He leaned forward once more. He removed his glasses and squinted at Teo's badge. "I see you're a veteran. If the Mutual Organization hasn't thanked you for your service, allow me to do so now."

"Well," said Teo, "thank you, sir."

The inspector smacked the table with an open hand. "I wasn't able to fight in the war. Allergies." He pinched his nose. "We owe this wonderful, amazing society we've built to the sacrifices made by men such as yourself."

SAME SONG, DIFFERENT BEAT (Sample Chapter)

"Well," Teo said again, "thank you, thank you. I appreciate that."

In a lower voice, the inspector said, "You owe it to yourself, soldier, to refrain from thinking too much." He tapped his finger against the side of his head. "Let's not forget how thinking led to the war in the first place. Such needless, horrific bloodshed. All because a few powerful people had differing opinions and refused to compromise."

On this, Teo could not have agreed more. He'd been young when the war started, but he'd been old enough to understand things might not go so well for him or others in his generation. The old men bickered. The young men duked it out. But these were negative thoughts, they only led to negative emotions. He promised the inspector he'd stop himself the moment he *suspected* he might start thinking.

"Amazing." Claud Ramirez slapped the table again and stood. "Wonderful. Just remember, we provide all the entertainment you need to occupy that space between your ears." This time, he pointed with two fingers to his eyes and then to Teo's eyes.

Teo took to his feet as well. "Yes," he said. "And it's amazing. Television, the radio. These things are wonderful, amazing."

The inspector rounded the table and patted Teo on his shoulder. "Now you're talking."

As they walked to the front of the store, Teo thought he noticed the inspector's smile vanish, for just a moment, as the inspector wished him well and said goodbye. He returned to the vegetable aisle to stack boxes. All the while, he kept his attention on the inspector. Claude Ramirez had, for some reason, felt the need to confer with Ji Young. They spoke in hushed voices. On several occasions, Ji Young looked over at Teo. She did not project anything he could interpret as positive or encouraging.

When the five o'clock alarm sounded from the charred Hollywood Hills, Ji Young put her hand on Teo's chest. Her bright, red fingernails must have cost her plenty. Most women seemed to spend their extra credits on such frivolous items. For whatever reason, they didn't cultivate desire for something as glorious as the Cheetah 3000. He felt the warmth of her body through her touch. It reminded him of the night they'd attempted recreational procreation. Despite her proximity, he still couldn't look her in the eye. He'd failed her, and the memory led to nothing but miserable thoughts. She said, "You need to watch your comments in public." If anyone understood the danger of revealing too much to other people, it would certainly be her. She told Teo, once, how she'd been a level seven after the war. When he asked her why she'd been demoted, she said she'd offered a superior an opinion she shouldn't have. She wouldn't reveal anything else. "That inspector is *very* suspicious. Whether you like 'Sunshine Manifesto' or not is irrelevant. That's the song we're allowed to play. Imagine stocking shelves without music in the background, how crowded your head would be with thoughts. Useless thoughts." When he opened his mouth to speak, she moved her hand from his chest to his lips. He tasted salt on her fingers. She said, "Thinking is the reason you couldn't please me, remember?"

This cut him like a blade jabbed into his throat and dragged to his belly. This Ji Young, this woman of such brutal honesty, differed so much from the boss Ji Young who roamed the aisles, day after day, offering the same, encouraging words to the workers ("You're doing a wonderful job. Amazing."). How did she separate these two people within her? He still wanted to make love to her and he knew she'd never give him a second chance. And why should she? Why should she risk it? Different night, same humiliation. "Okay," he finally said. "I'll keep my mouth shut."

"There's a good boy." She snagged a quick peek out the doors and then gave him a peck on the cheek. "I don't want you to have to go back to the garbage heap."

"Thank you." Did he blush as she wiped her lipstick from his face?

They walked to the corner to wait for a transport with the rest of the workers. The sun hadn't let up since the morning. Teo Paz stood still, a forced smile on his face, no different from anyone else around him.

Once he returned to his apartment, the ringing in his ear increased. With the rising volume came a hint of pain, like a needle, poking into his jawbone. He turned on the television hanging on the far wall of the living room. The Mutual News broadcast had already started. Pictures of smoggy, hazy, filthy, disgusting North California filled the screen. Wilma Minassian's voice narrated the usual story about misery beyond the border. "The tribes of Old San Fran," she said, "set fire to the Wharf district yet again." She said the unrest had resulted from lack of a central, organizing structure in the region.

Teo opened new boxes of powdered vegetables and powdered meat, mixed them in a bowl, and ran steaming water from the faucet in his tiny kitchen over the grains until they thickened into a brown sludge. He stirred it with a spoon and then sat down to watch the rest of the news. Same stories, different day.

As he finished his dinner, a sports program replaced the news. It must have been Wednesday. The game involved two teams attempting to throw a ball into a hole on their opponent's side of a gymnasium. The balls and the goals this week were smaller than the previous week's. Same game, different balls.

A crowd watching the competition cheered no matter which side scored. Teo could never keep track of who nabbed the most goals. At the end of each contest, both teams were declared winners by default. This kept everyone, the players and the audience, happy. No matter how loud the cheering got, however, Teo could not stop focusing on the ringing in his ear. He turned the volume on his television as high as it would go. He put his head next to one of the speakers on the bottom of the TV during a commercial for the Cheetah 3000. The engine roared, but it did not stop the siren wailing in the back of his mind. He focused on the actual Cheetah, a sleek cat capable of escaping anything, running, super-imposed, in the background of the commercial.

The latest version of the Minassian's situation comedy started after the sports program. Again, Teo jammed his ear against the speaker in hopes the laugh track would drown out the ringing. A headache developed. He could no longer sit on his plush, three-cushioned couch and watch television. He stormed out his door and through the hallway to a steel fire escape he often used as a balcony to enjoy the cool, South California night air. He caught himself on the railing and tried to slow his breathing. His vision doubled from the pounding down the center of his skull. On the sidewalk below, he thought he saw an inspector, just standing there, hands in the large pockets on the sides of his gray coverall, staring up at him, as though he knew him. Teo grabbed his forehead with his hands and squeezed. This gesture, he believed, would simmer the throbbing in his brain. It would align his vision. When he looked at the sidewalk once more, the man in the gray coverall had disappeared.

Read the rest of Ronin Heck's terrifying novella, *SAME SONG, DIFFERENT BEAT*, available wherever good books are sold!

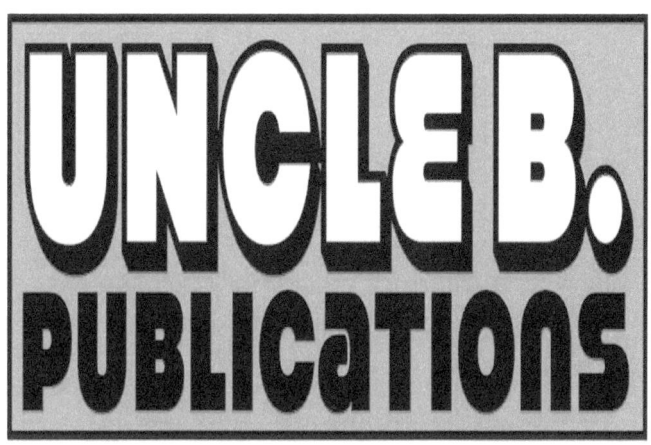

AN INDIANAPOLIS BASED
PUBLISHING MAFIA